BULL

{MEN'S FICTION}

BULL
{No. 1}

{Editor}

Jarrett Haley

{Managing Editor}

Jared Yates Sexton

{Editorial Board}

Lucas Ahlsen
Max Campbell
Michael Goodell
Ben Jahn
Ryan Ridge
Jon Trobaugh

{Editorial Assistants}

Maria Fahs
Troy Mathew
Josh Whitaker
Christopher Wolford

{Senior Editor}

Tim Chilcote

{Illustrations}

Patrick Haley
James-Alexander Mathers

{Reviews}

Curtis Dawkins

{Layout}

Jarrett Haley
Dan Azic

{Copyeditor}

Josh Whitaker

CONTENTS

Illustrations for "Houseboy", "Everything...", "New Baby"
and Klosterman by James-Alexander Mathers.
All others by Patrick Haley.

BULL logo by Dan Azic.

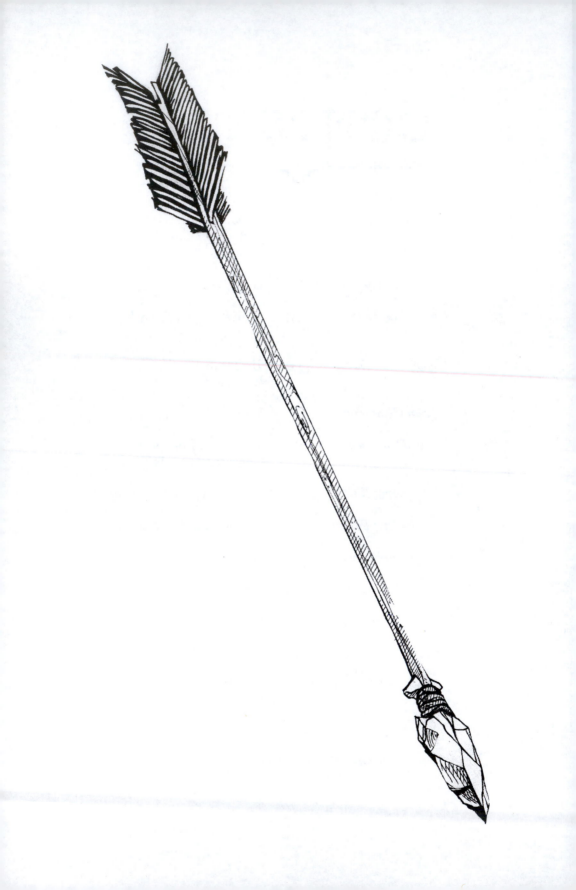

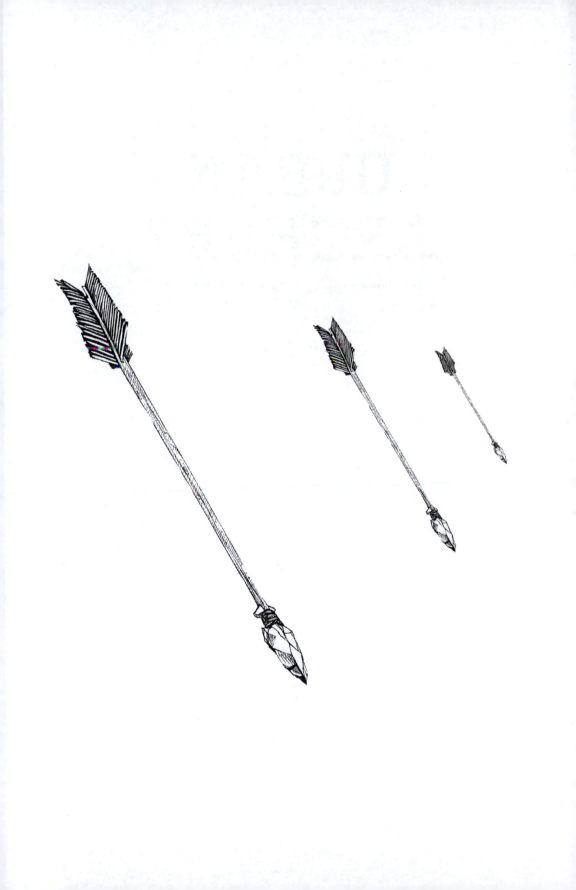

URBAN ARCHERY

Curtis Dawkins

ALL WEEK SOMEONE HAD been shooting arrows into my back-yard. I'd come out in the morning for the first smoke and cof-fee of the day, and in the dewy silver grass was one, sometimes two arrows stuck six inches into the ground at about a 70° angle. Arrows travel in a relatively straight line from point A to point B, I figured, especially in the calm of the night, so I had narrowed down the shooter's house to one of the four or five across parking lot of the Assembly of God, the distance of a football field away.

Most of the week I stood over my kitchen sink, looking out the window and wishing I had some binoculars. With binoculars I could probably spot some incriminating archery stuff leaning against one of the homes. I sure as hell wasn't going to go snooping around the backyards, and I didn't necessarily want to catch him or her in the act either.

While I was looking out my window I saw my neighbor Ter-rell hop my back fence. It's a chest-high fence but Terrell is some sort of ex-athlete, with his Air Jordans and perpetual sweats and everything. Occasionally when he and his wife had problems he'd take off before anything turned physical. He would hang out in my backyard until his wife Marvel cooled off. I watched him talk to himself for a little while, watched him light a cigarette and pace around some. Then I got concerned. The sun was nearly down and the arrows fell at night.

I slid open the glass door and called him over. "It's not safe out there," I said, and he stepped onto the small concrete porch and then into my house.

"You got that right," said Terrell, though I doubt we were talking about the same thing. He sat across from me at my dining room table and every now and then he'd glance nervously at the vertical blinds halfway closed across the quiet backyard.

It was his own fault his marriage was falling apart. Terrell felt bad about it and I think he really loved Marvel, but still, every other day when he got home from running his press at the paper factory, he'd hook up his bass boat to the back of his Dodge and meet his girlfriend at the little motel off the highway. Everyone knew about it; I don't even know why he bothered hooking up his glittery blue boat anymore. He never brought home any fish, and he never smelled like worms.

I popped open a couple beers and kept my eye on the backyard as he spoke. "I knew something was wrong when Marvel had a nice dinner fixed with meat and vegetables, some mac and cheese, baked potatoes and gravy."

"Sounds good," I said.

"Yeah, but I'm pretty sure the meat was Alpo." He took a long drink from the can of beer. "Or Mighty Dog. I found a little can with the label torn off."

Lights were popping on around the church and in the yards across the parking lot. I saw some movement near one of the house's swingsets, but it was only a dog digging a hole.

"With the gravy it was pretty good," Terrell said. "I kind of liked it."

"Isn't that something?" I said. "When I was a kid I ate a lot of dry dog food, but never the wet."

We sat there, the both of us.

"Actually, Terrell, I've got a little problem of my own that I want to run past you. You're an outdoorsman, right?"

I walked over to the closet between the kitchen and living room and took out the dozen arrows I'd collected there in a green glass vase of my ex-wife's. Together in a bunch they really looked as if they belonged in the vase, with thin wooden shafts and white synthetic feathers as fins; they looked like a bouquet of genetically-altered flowers from the future. I set them on the table in front of Terrell.

"Someone's been shooting these into my yard. I don't know what's going on—if they're kids or what. I think someone's trying to send me a message. From the way they stick in the ground, I've narrowed it down to one of those houses across the parking lot."

He picked all twelve of them up, seeming to weigh them. He lined a couple towards the light over the table, then he felt the metal tips with his index finger. "I don't think it's kids. You've got to have strength to pull a bow, to shoot an arrow that far."

I explained how they had been waiting for me in the morning—sometimes one, but more often two at a time.

Terrell took a drink of his beer and looked as if he was about to say something when we heard it: the hollow wooden sound of something hitting the concrete porch, then bouncing sharply off the sliding glass door. It couldn't have been anything but an arrow. I felt vindicated. You share a secret like that with a neighbor—and you never really *know* neighbors—but you say something like that and maybe he'll start thinking you're lonely, just making weird shit up for attention. It's very rare in life to share a strange secret like the arrows and have it verified immediately.

We rushed outside, and sure enough, in the yellow glow of my back porch light, there lay an arrow on the edge of the grass. Terrell looked up at the half-moon and I went to pick it up. "There might be more," I said. "Maybe we should go in."

Terrell and I looked across the parking lot and there he was, we saw him, what looked like a man waving down a car on a long stretch of 94. We walked over to the back fence. He made no attempt to shout at us, but only waved his arms, either trying to get our attention or warning us. Then he stopped waving, stooped to pick up something from the ground, and looked like he was fitting it into something else. Terrell and I ran inside, expecting at any second to feel the sting of an arrow flash through our backs. The feeling, I imagined, would be something medieval. We made it to the porch, then slid the door shut once we got inside. Terrell looked at me and smiled. "I've got his and hers bows in my garage if you want me to. They just need to be—"

"Get 'em," I said, and Terrell ran out the front door. I stood at the blinds and felt every single furious beat of my heart while Terrell was most likely digging through his garage, hunting for the remnants of what he probably once thought would be a good hobby he and Marvel could share.

I didn't see or hear the next one at all. I must have blinked or looked away for a moment because I found myself staring at new arrow shot fresh into the ground. In the porchlight the shaft seemed to glow and the feathered fins reminded me of a pale tulip. I was excited. With all the math I had in high school I figured that within a dozen shots I could put one in the guy's pocket.

Terrell walked in with the his and hers recurved bows and strung them up with bright white nylon bow-string by stepping on one end, bending the other down to the point where I thought it would snap, then tying off the end through a small hole. He held each bow by its end and waited for me to choose, all that energy drawn and ready to be released, like two snakes by the tails, like two waiting lives.

IN THE DAYROOM WITH STINKY

Curtis Dawkins

STINKY WALKS INTO THE room where the men play cards. They play dominos and talk. They play chess and sell homemade cards. They smoke in the corner by the window.

It smells like straight-up donkey ass in here, he says. Stinky thinks everything stinks. He says he's got extra-sensitive smelling and he doesn't smell nothin' good.

Stinky in the dayroom: Is that thunder in fucking October? The trees are changing. I think that one's dead though. These planes fly low because they're keeping an eye on me. When I leave, you watch—you won't see no more planes around here.

Stinky sits down across from me, lays a deck of cards on the table. He got some new T-shirts and what he really likes about them is that the tags have been removed, so it's impossible to put them on backwards. He was married—still is, technically—to a prostitute he calls Scared Sarah, who took her medication one night with a Wild Turkey chaser, and then the story gets fuzzy. The only indisputable fact is that she disappeared. Scared Sarah had a bad heart. Her teeth fell out because all the enamel was gone.

Nash is out of cigarettes, and his coffee's gone. He's at the next table and may have the flu. I would like to be able to see movies again. Charlie Kaufman wrote and directed a new one that I'll never see. I hate the loudness here. I sleep a lot. I wonder if the four guys playing their vampire role-playing game know that it isn't real? I don't think it's something they consider. I've gotten used to instant coffee. It's all right.

Most of my friends have killed someone. Most of my friends were notorious once. A couple of them you can see on *A&E's Cold Case Files*. Stinky's case shows half a dozen times a year. A guy behind me thinks my writing looks like Arabic. He locks in 92. I know because I take in laundry, then hand it out. I know where everyone locks. Almost. There are 240 men in this unit.

Is your name Sam? No. Good. I'll hang around killers but not pedophiles.

People talk way too much. No one cares what you have to say and I really think some people stay here or keep coming back because they like to talk and people on the outside are tired of listening to them. I heard Leonard Cohen say once that he spent five years in a monastery and he compared the experience to being a rough stone in a small cloth bag with other rough stones. The friction between the rocks turns all the stones to a flat shine. These guys, though, they don't think of prison that way. They think they're here by accident.

The hardest thing to get used to is the play fighting, learning the difference between real violence and two guys acting like kids. For the first couple of years you turn around at every loud noise.

What's the name of that card game you're playing? Casino, says Stinky. I mean solitary. You mean solitaire? And then he shuffles the deck, lays the cards in thirteen piles of four. He asks me what I think the odds are that there are four of a kind in one pile. About a million to one, I say. Then he turns over four aces in the first pile and all the rest in sequential order.

I should have been a card shark, he says. Hey, maybe if we showed that trick to the judge, he'd let us go.

Yeah, maybe.

I think the correct term is card *sharp*, but I've always thought card shark was the better description. I would rather be a shark than sharp, though I keep that to myself.

All the old grifters had names for the tricks they used: The Lefty Lucy, The Turn and Run, The Disappearing Deck, The Bloody Valentine, The Bootless Jack. And though Stinky knows a lot of card tricks, he has no names for any of them.

H ERE ARE THE FACTS of his case as reported to me by Stinky himself and Bill Kurtis of *Cold Case Files*:

Scared Sarah Brown neé Novak and Stinky are married in 1978. She wears white and he pays $50 for a nice, tall wedding cake, which she picks up and throws at him during the reception in the basement of the American Legion Post 714. The wedding gala is attended by a Who's Who of Kalamazoo County's dealers, pimps, and thieves. The marriage is rocky, and in a couple of years, it's completely on the rocks. There is a well-documented history of domestic incidents with the two of them alternating roles as the aggressor. She passes out nightly with a couple of Valium (she disliked the newer generation of benzodiazepines) and a half pint of Wild Turkey. He takes out a term life policy for $100,000, and a month later, she disappears. There is no body—no trace of a body found. Ever. Even to this day. The case goes cold with no insurance being paid because there's no proof Scared Sarah is dead and not in Cancun living on the beach. Six years later, some nutcase barfly named Monica "Deadeye" Silver says on the stand that Stinky told her all about how he smothered Scared Sarah, ran her through a meat grinder he used for venison, then fed her ground remains to a pen of thirty hogs north of town. Stinky says he has never even seen Monica. Her statement comes two weeks before the coroner was to pronounce Scared Sarah presumed dead, the insurance money paid to Stinky.

A brief legal primer: *corpus delecti* literally means "body of a crime." Generally, in a homicide case, there must be proof that someone died and that the deceased came to their end via foul play. Generally, it takes more than a recovered memory from a crazy woman to convict someone. But Michigan's funny that way.

Generally, it takes proof—unless $100,000 is involved, Stinky says. He thinks she most likely died en route south with a guy she probably barely knew. One day Stinky thinks she's in a ditch somewhere between Michigan and Mexico. Another day he thinks she's going to show up alive. Maybe here.

Also, I miss good music. I miss alternative music you can't hear on VH1.

Someone on B-wing took thirty of something. Thirty what? It don't matter, he took thirty of them. You take thirty of anything and that's a wrap. It's that time of the year. People get depressed. They think enough's enough.

When I get back to court, Stinky says, for my opening statement I'm gonna show the judge a razzle-dazzle card trick that's going to blow his mind.

You've got to come up with a catchy name for it, Stinky. You can't just say to him, Okay, Judge, here's my card trick.

He looks out the window. Snow is possible today, or tomorrow.

A name, huh?

Someone stands up: I'll tell you one thing; I'll tell you this—all that medication they got me waking up for at 5:30? They can stick it straight up their ass!

The one part of Stinky's story I always get hung up on is this: why get rid of her body if you're trying to collect insurance money? And this, too: he still seems stunned that she threw a beautiful $50 cake at him. It was thirty years ago.

Judge Peckerneck, for my opening statement, Stinky says he'll say, I'd like to call your attention to this deck of cards for a little something I call: Aces-in-the-Middle-Razzle-this-whole-thing-stinks-like-a-monkey-took-a-shit-in-an-old-boat-Dazzle.

Another thing I miss: when I would mow my yard, my dog followed close behind me, and when I would stop, he'd run into the back of my legs. There was something very comforting about that.

It's laundry day. I'm going to take a shower. On the way to lunch Stinky told me good things were going to happen to me today because he prayed for me and my kids for a long time last night. I'm going to take a shower then wait. I'm going to drink strong coffee and wait for good things to happen. Then again, there's that conveniently purchased insurance policy. Then again, there's no body.

A
NORTH

Curtis Dawkins

GEORGE WAS IN JAIL when his girlfriend Sunshine told him she had cancer. He couldn't touch her or hold her, of course, through the glass, through the phone. George and I were on A North, the suicide watch wing, in a 4-man cell. Just down the hall from us there were suicidal women who wrote dirty notes on little bars of Holiday Inn soap, then slid them to a stop in front of our cell. Our TV, mounted on the wall, was dying. Half the time there was only a black screen and the occasional haunting thump from the speaker.

No one died on the suicide watch wing when I was there. A man did commit suicide over in the jail, but he wasn't on A North, he was in segregation. My wife came to visit on the same day the jail officials handed his personal belongings to his grieving sister there in the waiting room. My wife didn't go into detail about it; she was shaken and I didn't press. But in my mind I've played that scene over and over again. I imagine a sibling, someone I love and grew up with, who goes to jail—which is bad enough—but then the personal demons set in and I never see them alive again. I clutch a paper bag that doesn't seem to weigh enough.

On A North, no one died. None of us, at least. George's girlfriend had cancer though, and we all felt horrible about it. When you're separated from the people you know and love, every emotion is multiplied. Your mind becomes a very clear prism, where every feeling enters in, then becomes seven or eight different shades. We were all responsible for being there, of course. But that only makes you feel worse when you're the one in jail.

We were sad about Sunshine, and we were worried about George, who was a surly kid that would fight anyone at the drop of a hat. Finding out about the cancer didn't help his already touchy mood.

I had been making chess pieces from wet toilet paper. I was finishing the bishops, which were turning out to look exactly like the pawns. Then George said, Her hair was falling out. And then he began to cry. I mean he really cried. Sobbing I guess you'd call it.

How long has she had cancer? one of us asked.

She just —sob— found out —sob— today —sob.

And of course, being the resident know-it-all, I explained to George that something was strange about Sunshine's cancer story. No one's hair falls out the same day they're diagnosed with cancer.

That's the chemo, I said. And she couldn't have started chemo yet.

I told you before about how violent George was; his father used to set up fights between him and his drinking buddies' kids. They would place bets, like the kids were roosters or dogs. I honestly expected to be punched after I'd basically called Sunshine a liar. But I wasn't punched, I just kept adding my wet wads of toilet paper to build up the bishops.

George stopped sobbing and he watched the black TV as if he could see what was happening there.

I always assumed it was Sunshine who was the liar, but years after I was on A North with George, it occurred to me that it was probably him who had made the whole story up. For sympathy, or something like it.

He sat there watching the black screen and seemed to really enjoy the soap opera that was going on. It was like a radio play, or eavesdropping, as if the action were taking place just on the other side of our cinderblock wall. There was a hostage situation—some nut with a Southern accent demanding a couple million in ransom. We could hear that the hostage was a regular, so nothing permanently bad was going to happen to her. She might think she's going to die, but she wasn't going to. In fact, the situation might do the spoiled twerp some good. It might deepen her shallow soul. Then there was the loud thump from the speaker and a wisp of smoke rose from the back of the TV. And that was it. The television died a slightly smoky death.

We never got to find out how the hostage situation turned out, if it affected the soap opera's character or not. I like to think it gave her nightmares. I like to think there were numerous nightmare hostage sequences where she woke up screaming on her canopy bed, not knowing for sure whether she was still tied to that cheap chair in the warehouse, or simply tangled up in her own sheets.

HOUSE BOY

Sara Lippmann

I AM WORKER FOR STRICKLAND. They call me houseboy. This is true: I watch house. But I am man, I have twenty-three year, I serve as officer in Tzava, this is Israeli army, I travel to Thailand, Laos, India, Vietnam, Indonesia, I smoke the hashish on lazy bitch and acquire radical armband tattoo, I make the little repair. Press caulk tipping to hermit the window and squeeze; it is like fucking. Strickland have nice country house in Bucks County, PA but he does not give shit for insect. I execute the ant of red fire. They do not molest me. They run for a meaningless life. I exclaimate, Die ant! I paint the fence, the baseboard. I am not electrical. In Strickland family there is loaded money, nice mansion house. I sleep in bunker. Do you know how to make *beitzim* in microwave oven? I also eat cornflakes.

They have massive lawn, maybe 20,000 meter. They have a tractor for haircuts on Thursday. They have Olympic-size swimming pool!

Strickland family have pool worker to measure the fever but I skim leaf and fly with net like Trojan condom. This duty I perform most excellent even when Strickland is away in big city because excellent is first and foremost. Without duty there is *balagan*. Houseboy! They funny me. *Ma pitom!* I say, You funny me. They say: No, Avital. You are saver the life. There is God in my name, you believe it. There is also father and the pitiful droppings of dew. I adjust the house fever to 21 centigrade. I thirsty the plants. Without you, Strickland say, would be *balagan*.

All week is quiet. I hear birds. I hear insect legs rubbing like violin bow. I ride skateboard from son of Strickland to town called Main Street. There is WaWa convenience store. I shop. This is what I buy: hot dog, pickle, pretzel; I buy Slim Jim, noodle soup exploding like sponge in hot water. I buy beera in cans and put them in my sack and skate the board home. When you are alone your mind can go to crazy but I tempt not to go there. It is safe in Bucks County, PA. Sometime there is deer eating the hydrangea bush and sometime I exclaimate, Die deer! But sometime I stand there and say, you are my friend, deer, you have eyes like hand grenade, when I vision your blood pulsating true animal vein make me want to be a better man.

For weekends I put the lounge cushion out. I bring the cushion in when it rains or such weather. I sit outside the pool. It is very rich! Strickland territory have light sensitive as spies for motion detection. Make yourself at home, Strickland say after I carry equipage so I am to make very comfortable. There is no care in the world! At night everything is awesome and pacifist. Water shimmers like the scale of fish and sometime I think of Tzipi. She works for car dealer in Haifa, she sells the Peugeot gently used but I desire the fantasy love and what we have, what we had, is sex. The fucking. Her mother have jelly arms in total vibration like the ass of Britney Spears. I love Britney Spears! I also love Pearl Jam, White Wedding song by Billy Idol, Red Hot Chili Peppers. Blood sugar baby. There is a bounty of forgetful CDs in a brown box down in the bunker where I dig them from Strickland son and play radical tunes on digital radio alarm clock.

Let me explain you something, I tell Tzipi. I don't tell her classified but she has her own secrets. This is the way of life—who knows nothing? It is good, the fuck, it used to went plenty, but now I am affirmative: fucking is not enough. What will happen when you get sick and fat? She throws shoe at my head. Ars! I duck. What is this bullshit? I am not even *arsim*. But Tzipi is true. Everyone funnies me: Who is making such time for love fantasy? Americans are wild for fantasy, so I come to U.S. for summer. Strickland family are good people and very lovish with wine at parties.

There is much items to fix. I take my hammer to pool deck. When I vision a lonely nail I hammer that nail because Mrs. Strickland worries the tetanus emergency. Then—how do you say?—I light up the pool deck. My fire glows green breakthrough to other side. My fire is a Pink Floyd song. I love Pink Floyd! I smoke Marlboro. I think. I try thinking English. I try to dream in English but in dream wild beasts rush the humble mountaintop like refuges to Yam Suf. A stampede of zebra and giraffa and peacock. The pool makes hypnotic on me. The wind blows, the water gleam the color the eyes of Tzipi when she wear blue contact lens. I swim Olympic. I swim and swim without thought or molesting.

Tonight the sister of Strickland have come for visit. She wears tight bodice with horny nipple and her hair tied in bread like dancer. She has long neck like dancer but she is not young like dancer but old like cougar town. She is call Bette and there is God in her name, too. She repose the guest quarter above my head and I am quiet, I hear the padding of feet, I smell lemon soap ventilation, I am mouse in bunker. She is no sister. Basement, she whispers me.

Please, to listen: At the table I chew silent as fucking Mossad. I vision Bette. There is something shell shockage about her. She does not flutter the eyelash. Her lips they are a wire fence. On Friday Strickland have housemaid but Bette say she must to clean her own goddamn cup. I leave my plate—I am a man feeling the home like Strickland—I leave everything and go to pool calling my name like round rosy ass of virgin. Bette is at the sink soaping. Through the window I hear Strickland: Lighten up! Why must you be all the time thinking? I sit. I massage the cushion. I smoke through the glowing sensation. What am I doing? I look out the pool and up the sky. There are stars. I connect the dot. Bette has shoulders ripe as Jericho orange from once upon a time. I do not go there. Where do I go? The whole world is cry. Water flood her cup, spill her wrist, soften the elbow, I drain in tears, but when she close the tap to breathe I pray maybe she have place deep inside lung for me.

EVERY-THING FAR AWAY UP CLOSE

Nick Bertelson

GRANDPA BUB GREW UP in a generation without alcoholics. There were plenty of winos, boozers, lushes and drunks, but that was back when alcohol had personality; it was your drinking that defined you. The winos drank together and the boozers drank alone, the lushes drank what others had and the drunks drank whatever. But I don't have to tell any of you that. This isn't my first time here either.

They called Grandpa Bub a moonshiner, and in my eyes that

made him a craftsman. He spent days out in the woods tending to his still, holed up under the tarpaulin he'd strung between two birch trees. He may have thought it was hidden, but all you had to do was follow the garden hose that ran from the back spigot. That's what I did anyway, and I'd go check out his rig of two propane burners, a big copper coil, clumpy brown bags of God knows what, and a stack of old Penthouses. What he cooked out there made his clothes smell like the ammonia farmers put on their fields before the dirt froze. Made his breath smell flammable. If any of you ever had moonshine, you know the smell I'm talking about.

In the winter of 1980 I'm guessing Grandpa Bub had just turned sixty. It was the year he dragged seventy feet of barbed-wire fence down main street at two in the afternoon, the same year the county magistrate installed what had to be the first breathalyzer ever made into Bub's truck. It sat on the floorboard, big as a microwave, so big it kept the shifter from going into fourth gear. It had to be ten times the size of the ones they got now. I'm sure some people here know them well—the one I got now is black and sleek. I've seen them get smaller and smaller over the years. Same car, different breathalyzer: that's my story.

People ask me if I blame Bub for my drinking, but the word blame is too easy a thing to throw around. You can pack as many people as you want under that word until it becomes more of a pitiful excuse than a pitiful reason. Grandpa Bub was a craftsman at least. He made his product from scratch and enjoyed it. He said his sweat and blood went into that stuff and he meant it in more ways than one. I think of that every time I throw a case of King Cobra into the trunk of my car. Two of them to get through Sunday.

And Grandpa Bub at least drank with Karl, our neighbor down the road, Bub's apprentice of sorts. Karl was a lot closer to my age than Bub's, but for nineteen, he had built up a tolerance beyond his years. The two of them got to drinking especially hard when they went hunting. By hunting, I mean they drove around the county shooting rabbits out the truck window. I got to go along by virtue of my breath. Grandpa Bub called me his "Trumpet Man"—it was my job to blow in the breathalyzer and keep the truck running. Bub always drove, never once got in a car unless he was behind the wheel. But back then, if it wasn't for me he wouldn't have gone anywhere.

THEY LOADED THE TRUCK with everything they needed: guns, ammo, and moonshine, maybe a mason jar or three. They had two guns between them. Grandpa Bub with his over-and-under .410 and Karl with a .17 rifle. They loved to argue guns. Karl complained about rabbits full of shot from the .410, saying he near breaks a tooth every time. Grandpa Bub would make a show of taking out his false teeth. "I ain't got nothing to worry about!" he said. He thought that was real fun. Karl and me would do our best to laugh and try not to look at Bub's grey, slug-like gums.

We'd ride the back roads watching for bunnies in the ditches, picking out their gray fur from shadows in the snow. They passed the jar of shine back and forth and I blew the trumpet. I'd blow once to get the truck started and every half-hour or so afterward; it was the beep that let you know. That thing would start beeping and Bub would get all excited—"Come on, Satchmo, fill them cheeks!" He held the hose up to my mouth and his fingers fluttered like he was working the valves.

"Rabbit!" Karl said, cranking down his window. He spotted them most the time.

Grandpa Bub dropped the hose.

"Stop the truck, Bub. There's a rabbit back there."

So he stopped and we all looked in the rearview to make sure the warden wasn't around. Karl loaded his .17, flipped the safety, and hung it out the truck window.

"You keep that other eye open," said Bub, "or I'll stick my finger in it."

"It's open, old man."

Grandpa Bub, for some reason, shot with both eyes open and felt everyone should do the same.

Like a sickness, an awful silence always settled in my chest before a gun fired. It always seemed louder than the shot—that silent wait that sounded through everything. Karl fired, then opened the door and stumbled down the bank into the ditch. The rabbit writhed on its back, and Karl twisted its head off right there. I could see its long feet still kicking as he walked back. Blood dripped to the snow.

"Another gut-shot," Karl said at the door. "Crap-bag broke."

"I don't know why you use that thing," said Bub. "Just use the four-ten and get it over with."

"I'd shoot them with a Daisy before a shotgun." Karl threw the limp rabbit into the truck-bed. "Ain't much sport shooting from a truck window anyway."

Karl said that all the time but there's no chance either one of them could hunt like real hunters. They weren't ever going to walk through the woods with snowshoes on their feet. After an hour they probably couldn't stand much less walk, and the cab that had started out full of back-slapping and chatter would grow silent, both of them lost to their own thoughts and me in the middle, breathing into the hose.

We got up into the hills and found a Level-B with no tracks on it. Bub loved being the first to cut through the snow on these back roads, where the snow blew sideways through the middle of nowhere. The drifts along the road would sometimes be taller than the truck and the trees reached out of them like hands. When we'd get high enough on a hill, I'd look out and see a desert of snow.

"Might see a quail covey down in the brush," Karl said.

"Don't even think about asking for my four-ten. You can shoot each one of them with your seventeen." Grandpa Bub laughed and I laughed too, but I didn't understand guns enough to be sure what was funny.

"Slow the truck," Karl whispered. The way he spoke I thought he spotted the nose of a patrol car up behind the roadside scrub.

"Slow down, Bub!"

Karl slapped the dash this time and I saw why. Far up the road, I caught it just for an instant: a flash of gray I figured too big for a rabbit, could've been the head of a bobcat, maybe—if the rest of its body was hunkered down in the snow, I mean. But then I saw the ears like paddles, and I knew.

"That," said Karl, "is a fucking jackrabbit."

It sprang off the road then and ran so far up the ditch only Karl could track him. He was leaning halfway out the window to keep sight of it and nearly fell out when Bub finally ground the truck to a stop.

"He went to your side," Karl said. "I'm getting out." He grabbed in the back for his gun case. Grandpa Bub threw the truck into neutral.

"Hold up now," he said. "You let Buddy have this one."

"No way I'm giving up that rabbit to a kid," said Karl. "That thing was huge!"

"He won't have a problem hitting him then. Buddy shoots lefty; he's got the angle on it."

I did shoot left, but not at all by choice. It was Grandpa Bub taught me how to find my good eye—you overlap your fingers and thumbs and make a hole between your hands, then focus on something in the hole and bring your hands up to each eye. The one that keeps focus without your hand blocking, that's the strong eye, or dominant, they call it. I was left-eye dominant, so I had to shoot with my left arm, which I never have gotten used to. I wanted my right so badly; I must have pulled my hands to my face a hundred times. I wanted my right one because I knew that if I was hunting with Grandpa Bub, I'd have to sit on his lap to shoot anything.

"You get up here, Buddy," he said, cranking down the window. "Use the rifle. It's a got a scope."

"Jesus," said Karl. "My rabbit with my gun. Suppose I'll dress it and cook it and serve it to him on a platter, too." He had a plug of tobacco in his lip that made him look all the more angry. "And after all the bitching you do about my seventeen. Hell no, Bub. I don't think so."

But Grandpa Bub reached for the gun.

"I said no, old man!" He swatted Bub's hands off the zipper of his gun case. That's when Bub smacked Karl straight in the mouth.

The way both of them sat there staring at each other, breathing, I felt barely there. It felt like the moment before a gunshot, and I knew that moment was bigger than me, bigger than Karl, bigger than the jackrabbit, even. Bub pointed a finger in his face.

"The next time you want moonshine, you drive up to Whitey Mitchum's and he'll make you pay for it. More than I ever did, any-way."

I'd never known money to change hands between them. That much was a fact.

Karl's eyes went from Bub, to the Mason jar, then they went far out his window. He didn't look once at me. Even as he handed me the gun case.

"That's what I thought," Bub said, squinting down the ditch for the rabbit in the snow. "Come on, Buddy, get up here." I didn't want to get on his lap, not after he smacked Karl, not ever. I shook my head.

"C'mon!" said Bub, "I don't bite!" I imagine he all but lifted me up like a baby and set me on his warm thigh. Karl stared out his window still, having nothing of it. "You set that gun out there," Bub said, softly. His hot breath filled my ear. It smelled foul and bitter. If there's anything I remember it was that smell. And I knew that when we got home, he would make me have the last swig off the mason jar. He did that when I didn't have to blow into the trumpet anymore. I can't remember the taste, but I do remember how the heat set on my lips and pumped through my temples, and then that looseness all over, like your arms and legs just came unscrewed a little.

It wouldn't be the first drink I took off Grandpa Bub, whether he knew it or not. And like I said, it's not Grandpa Bub I blame for my drinking. And I don't blame Karl for anything either, even though he's the one who kept up the still after Bub died, the one who gave me pills for the first time and pretty much everything beyond that. I'm guessing some of you all probably knew Karl too, from when he worked over at the Dairy Sweet takeout window, how you'd drive over the cord and make the bell ding inside, then go back over it again so he knew it was you. I know Karl's got his own problems now and he might blame Bub, I guess. I never knew enough about what went on between them, really. For all I knew, back then they were just a couple of drunks shooting rabbits from a truck.

Karl turned back from the window. He asked me: "Do you even see him?" He was talking about the rabbit.

I didn't say anything.

"Answer, boy," Bub said. "You see him or not?"

I said nothing. I saw nothing. Just snow and maybe some dots of rabbit shit, a lot of it everywhere. Maybe it was Karl wanting to smooth things over with Bub, or maybe he just wanted his rifle to be responsible for killing a jackrabbit, but he grabbed the barrel and moved it to the right spot for me. With the scope at my eye, everything blurred and whizzed past, and when it stopped it all came into focus. There was the jackrabbit: his ears huge and maraca-shaped. They glowed orange from the sun hitting them, and in the scope I even saw red veins running all through them. I watched him breathing in the crosshairs.

"Open that other eye," Bub said.

When I opened my closed eye—the right one, the weak one I couldn't make dominant—a tension formed in my head. In one eye sat the rabbit, still in the crosshairs, and the other was blurry with all the stuff around me I couldn't see. I shot and I hit it, that's all I know. If Karl went to get it after, if he twisted off its head and gutted it there on the road, if we ate it that evening or let it freeze in the night like we did most rabbits, ruining the meat since the fur was still on, the guts still inside—I wish I could tell you, but I can't remember. I suppose that's what I'm trying to say, and that may be the reason why I'm here. Because to me, that rabbit is everything but dead.

THE HEART IS A STRONG INSTRUMENT

Jon Morgan Davies

B Y SATURDAY THE FAD was already on the decline. It had reached its zenith on Thursday, when Jewlia_Looey_Dryfuss_38, on Letterman, threw a knife in the air and caught the blade in her mouth. Then twelve-year-olds started doing it, and Regis on his morning show, and if nothing evolved further, it wouldn't have been more than a week before the whole thing got cheesy and fell into oblivion like so many other things had.

But at the time of the party that Friday, the fad was still current enough that none of us felt self-conscious about giving into it.

When we arrived that evening, the floor as usual belonged to my girlfriend, Janice_Bodiceripper. We were at Brian_M_325's place, a condo he'd purchased from me two months earlier. Brian had used the interior decorator I'd recommended, and the result was something like a 1950's science-fiction torch lounge: skyline view and body-stockinged poster girls, mixed drinks and floor-to-ceiling mirrors, Spanish peanuts and smokes aplenty.

Janice seized the spotlight as soon as we walked through the door. It's what I loved about her. She shimmied about the apartment's living room, grinding her hips, showing off her belly and the sides of her waist. She'd brought her own knife and held the blade in her mouth like a pirate. All twenty-six eyes were upon her, waiting to see how far she'd go, how far she could go.

There's only so much one could do in this world. With a body like hers, and in the three months I'd been with her, I'd just about seen and done all that I could. We'd hugged and kissed and I'd seen down her cleavage, but that was all. Janice's performance now was pretty tame by our standards, so I aimed myself toward the kitchen for a beer. There was no talking to her when she was in the mood to entertain, and I wanted to check out what Brian had done with the cabinets. Being in real estate, I often found these things mattered.

I'd just plucked a Bud from the fridge when Karen_Loves_U69 walked into the kitchen.

Karen_Loves_U69: why aren't u with janice?

Sometimes I thought Karen had a thing for me, the way she'd always show up at the parties and bars I went to, the same stores and live tutorials. It didn't help that Janice often invited her, or told her where we'd be. Karen was a bore.

HouseGuy_42: getting a drink. want one?

Karen_Loves_U69: do i look like i need one?

HouseGuy_42: you'd know more than i would

Karen_Loves_U69: my life level is fine but if i don't have to pay...

HouseGuy_42: it's a party. brian prepaid

Karen_Loves_U69: ok

Karen was also a freeloader, didn't pay for anything. Most freeloaders disappeared after a couple of weeks. There was only so much one could do without paying. Most people got bored—or quit once their life started to nosedive and they had to start working or searching for free food. But Karen kept on, a scavenger. I knew she'd never buy any property. She was a waste of my time. But I was too nice not to talk to her.

And most importantly, Janice liked her. She'd even invited Karen out to dinner once at our expense. That was the night Karen told us her husband had recently left her, only I couldn't tell which life she was talking about. The way Janice consoled her and glorified me, it seemed like she was trying to set Karen and me up. A true mooch, Karen left right after the meal, but Janice and I stuck around.

Janice_Bodiceripper: next time u should ask for her phone number

HouseGuy_42: but i'm dating you

Janice_Bodiceripper: only for now. she seems to need somebody. maybe even irl

HouseGuy_42: i'd rather just date you

Janice was fun. Dating her was how I'd always imagined dating a stripper would be. She wasn't a stripper, of course—that sort of thing wasn't allowed here. But she came as close as she could: wet T-shirt contests, G-strings on the beach, mud wrestling. I kept hoping Janice would agree to meet in person, but she always put me off. I wondered if she had another boyfriend. She said no but was coy about it. It didn't really seem possible given how much time we spent together.

One day, she kept saying.

Stealing was another thing not allowed, which meant free accounts couldn't touch food or drink unless it was purchased or given to them. I opened the fridge, pulled out a Budweiser, and handed it to Karen.

Karen_Loves_U69: now i remember why i dont drink

HouseGuy_42: he's got corona

Karen_Loves_U69: since when?

HouseGuy_42: new marketing agreement--read yr email

I traded her Bud for a Corona.

Karen_Loves_U69: any lime?

HouseGuy_42: yeah

I opened the fridge again and pulled out a little green orb. The graphics weren't too sophisticated on it yet, a sign Sunkist still hadn't paid for product placement. But it was a lime, and that was enough. I took out my pocketknife, quartered the lime, and handed her a chunk.

Karen_Loves_U69: can i see that?

She meant the knife. I gave it to her, and she did as I expected: threw it over her head and caught the handle with her teeth. Nothing special. I'd have rather watched Janice.

Then Karen lunged forward. The knife sunk into my heart. Blood spurted from my chest like welding sparks. In the mirror I could see the gash and the blood running red down my shirt.

HouseGuy_42: how'd u do that?

Karen_Loves_U69: lol i don't know lol

I was a successful man. I kept my life at a steady one hundred. The blood poured out of me onto the kitchen floor, and I fell to sixty-eight. I ran, or tried to run, into the living room. I wanted to show Janice and the others. But Karen stabbed me again, in the back.

Karen_Loves_U69: lol

My life lost another thirty-two points. I dropped to the floor. My legs stopped moving, even though I pushed forward.

HouseGuy_42: somethings wrong

At least I could still talk.

Karen_Loves_U69: !!! the blood the way it gushes out did u see that?

She stabbed me again.

HouseGuy_42: STOP

I was down to seven. My words came out slowly.

Karen_Loves_U69: i didn't know u could do this here

HouseGuy_42: u can't

Or at least you couldn't. Before this, suicide had been the only option, and that only by disappearance. Whole new vistas were opening up. Possibilities for war and terrorism, extortion and muggings and carjackings and dictatorships. Maybe we'd finally be able to have sex. Make babies. New families and loved ones. I thought of Janice and how it might be here just like it was everywhere else.

But kill people on a free account?

It didn't seem fair. I'd paid. I'd paid and I worked hard to keep up my points so that I wouldn't have to pay again. I was even making a little money on the side, through the real estate ventures. I was making something of myself. I was almost self-supporting in real life. A month or two more, I figured, I'd be able to go full time.

HouseGuy_42: my connection is messed up

Karen_Loves_U69: u want me to get janice? the others?

HouseGuy_42: yes

HouseGuy_42: and 911

But Karen had already left. The room was empty except for me. I looked at myself in the mirror, the blood smeared across my face. Had I missed an e-mail?

I queried Admin. The sidebar opened, but it was blank. Everything was running slow.

Janice_Bodiceripper: what happend, houseguy?

Janice was kneeling over me. She was topless. Topless! And gorgeous. I'd missed it, the moment when she discovered herself, and in front of so many others. Janice's breasts hung over my face. I wanted to touch them. I wanted to touch them so much, but I couldn't raise my hands.

HouseGuy_42: stabbed

Karen_Loves_U69: i stabbed him. want to see it again?

HouseGuy_42: no

Brian_M_325: he looks sick

Janice_Bodiceripper: it let me take off my top

HouseGuy42: yes :) help

Brian_M_325: i think we're losing him

Janice_Bodiceripper: we can't

But Brian was right. My life was down to three. My vision was fading, colors losing contrast. I had to act.

HouseGuy_42: #?

Janice_Bodiceripper: what?

HouseGuy_42: phone #?

Karen_Loves_U69: he wants your phone #--u know how he always liked you

Janice_Bodiceripper: i can't

Brian_M_325: don't be a prude

Brian_M_325: not now

Brian_M_325: he's dying

Janice_Bodiceripper: but he can't die

Brian_M_325: oh but he is

My life fell to two.

HouseGuy_42: #

Janice_Bodiceripper: u don't want to meet me, not in real life

HouseGuy_42: yes

Janice_Bodiceripper: i'm a guy

HouseGuy_42: ?

Brian_425_M: but yr avatar

Janice_Bodiceripper: is an avatar

Karen_Loves_U69: woh--i thought for sure u were a woman

Janice_Bodiceripper: thanks

I was down to one. I couldn't speak. I didn't care.

Janice_Bodiceripper: sorry houseguy--i never meant it to go this far

Brian_425_M: she's a man, man!

Karen_Loves_U69: i mean the way you talked to me about my husband

Janice_Bodiceripper: i have a wife and 2 kids

Brian_M_425: that's sick

Karen_Loves_U69: it's like u knew all about divorce, about men cheating

Janice_Bodiceripper: i'm sorry

My life had stabilized. Now it was going up. I was at three, four, five.

HouseGuy_42: stab me

Janice_Bodiceripper: i'm sorry really i am

HouseGuy_42: stab me

Karen_Loves_U69: watch this

Janice_Bodiceripper: no

Karen_Loves_U69: this is so cool

Blood gushed from my back, from between my ribs. It gushed and gushed and filled the floor. But no matter how many times she stabbed me, the world would not let me go.

VENTURA

Ryan Glenn Smith

THE PONTIAC HAD BEEN a project of mine for a while. I had taken out the original 307 motor, which had about 150,000 miles on it, and put in a 454 from the rusted-out Chevelle SS my stepdad left in the garage. He'd be pissed, but he's also locked up for a while, so I wasn't worried. The Ventura is basically the same car as a Chevy Nova, and mine was a '71, mostly black except the hood still primer gray. I needed to finish painting it but I was broke from the transmission. Needed a new radio too, the AM/FM dial was lousy and wouldn't pick up much of anything. But the car was fast with that big engine in there.

Reggie never was that good a friend of mine, but he knew I spent a lot of time working on the car. He had an apartment not far from where I lived with my mom. She'd been having a hard time with Dale locked up, and I was happy to stay with her and save rent. Reggie would come around the house every now and then wearing his backpack, looking like an overgrown school kid. He'd drop by to talk and bum cigarettes, probably because I smoke Winstons and he only had generics. He always asked me about the car, how fast it would go. He said he had a Camaro once but totaled it drag racing after a pint of Jack. He didn't have his license anymore and he could never hold down a job. He'd work a couple of weeks doing construction, get paid in cash one day, wind up in jail that night.

But lately he'd been good. He cut his hair short and got a job at Jimbo's doing oil changes. He'd been there six weeks I think, so I figured he'd reformed. Reggie came to me one day asking for a ride.

I was smoking on the porch when he walked up in his ratty jeans and bust-up sneakers. I knocked one out of my pack because I didn't want to hear him ask again. "Thanks," he said, scratching at his scruffy neck like a dog. "How's the Ventura runnin' today?"

"Just fine. I got the tranny shifting real smooth now. No slips."

He clicked his tongue against his teeth. "Bet you could get it up to a hundred real quick."

"Racing ain't my thing."

"Well amigo, I got paid today. You mind runnin' me to my bank?"

He shifted under his backpack, which was kind of slung over his right shoulder. I always figured Reggie to be the type of guy who'd cash a check at the liquor store. But I had the day off and nothing else to do. "Guess not," I said. "What bank you use? First America?"

"Naw, I'm at Heritage, over there on Cheatham."

"Well just let me get my wallet. I want to get a sandwich while we're over there."

"Hey that's fine, buddy," he said. "Tell you what, I'll buy you lunch for the ride."

I didn't expect Reggie to be a generous guy either, but I wasn't one to refuse a meal. We got in the car and I fired up the engine. "That's got a good sound," he said, pounding his fist on the dash. "Let's see how fast we can get this thing goin'!"

I kind of sped through the neighborhood but I didn't go as fast as he probably wanted to. It was summer and there was kids running around. We hit the main strip and he kept pushing on me to gun the car faster and faster. And I did go fast, faster than I usually would, but I knew my car would do a lot better out on the highway. I should've been worried about getting a ticket, but something about Reggie made me feel like I could do anything I wanted and get away with it.

We got across town pretty quick. I started to pull into this barbecue shack, but Reggie asked me to take him to the bank first. Outside the bank Reggie said to just pull up by the door. "I'm just running in and out," he said. "You can wait here." He grabbed his backpack and left the door open. I turned on the radio and looked at my watch. It was 3:56, Friday afternoon.

It was goddamn hot in the vinyl seat and I had to squirm around to keep from sticking. I messed with the radio and found an Allman Brothers song, lit a cigarette and looked out at the road. There wasn't too much traffic even at this hour. I was hungry. All I wanted was some pulled pork with slaw on it and a large sweet tea.

It really shouldn't have surprised me to see Reggie run out the bank with a stuffed garbage bag in one hand and a bigass pistol in the other. It really shouldn't have surprised me at all, but goddamn it did.

"Are you fucking serious?" I yelled at him.

He jumped in the car. He was smiling the whole time. "Come on, Barry! We gotta go!"

"What the fuck, Reggie!"

"Ain't no time for that, man," he shouted. "Move your ass!"

I threw the car into drive and sped out into traffic. I could hear a cop siren already in the distance, so I gunned it straight out of town and soon there wasn't much around us at all but the pines.

"Hey Barry," Reggie started, ass-up and looking through the rear window even though there was nothing to see. "I'm like Butch Cassidy, and you're the Sundance Kid!"

"What the hell you thinking, Reggie? Getting me mixed up in this?"

"You got the car, man. What else you need this fast-ass car for?"

"How about getting to work?"

"We won't have to work one day more after this."

"You didn't shoot nobody, did you?"

He sat back down and lit up one of his generics. "Course not, man. It's just to scare 'em, is all. It's all old-timey, see, but it still works. You want me to shoot it?"

"Fuck no. Where'd you get that?" Thing looked like it was straight out of the Civil War.

"Got a buddy at work." Reggie set the gun down on floorboard and opened the bag. There was a lot of money in it. I had no idea how much and I don't think Reggie did either. I'd always figured he'd go down for robbing a convenience store over sixty bucks or something. Not something like this.

"They get all the deposits from restaurants and businesses and shit like that. Over there at the Heritage Bank."

"Christ, Reggie…"

"I knew they was about to get all their cash out for the truck. I'd cased the place, you know, I took this real serious. I'd checked it out and knew if I got there right then I'd just have to walk in looking all tough and shit and tell them what to do."

I listened to him go on about how goddamn smart he was for twenty minutes, speeding through the countryside and passing the two or three cars that wound up in front of me. I thought about how I'd get arrested and wind up in prison, right next to my stepdad, how he'd yell at me through the bars and give me all kinds of hell about the Chevelle SS. I thought about my mom all alone. I thought about turning us in, turning Reggie in.

"We gotta get rid of that money, Reggie. What if it's got one of those paint-bombs in it or something?"

"Naw," he said. "I was watching them when they put it in there. I saw em try it with some kind of dye thing like you're talkin' about. But I told her if she put that shit in there, I'd come back and rape her and kill her."

He was probably serious, I thought. I mean—I'm sure he said it, but now I wondered if he really meant it, because I couldn't put nothing past him anymore. I didn't say anything for at least thirty or forty more miles. It was too loud in the car anyway with hot wind blowing through the windows. I just watched the needle vibrate around a hundred, watched the afternoon flicker in and out of the trees. If I had been alone or with anybody else, I might have actually enjoyed myself.

WE CAME UP ON a little unincorporated town. I slowed down when the signs dropped the speed limit in steps from fifty-five to thirty. There was a diner and a motel there—one of those empty, family-run, small-town joints. I told Reggie I was hungry even though it was a lie. My stomach was all knotted up. "How about you buy me some lunch now?"

There were two semis parked at the side of the diner near the motel. The lot was empty except for those big rigs and my Ventura. I started to park away from the buildings so I could take off at high speed if I needed to. Then I thought, I ain't making no goddamn getaway; I'll come out hands-up if I have to. I parked nose-in right against the window. "You think they're gonna know it's us in there, Reggie? You think they'll know it was you?"

"These folks don't know shit," he said. "Probably one cop in this whole town. Barney-fuckin-Fife with his one bullet in his shirt pocket." He put the pistol under the seat and left the car carrying the bag of money. "Open up the trunk for me," he said, pounding on the metal. I'd taken all the locks off when I was painting and I told him so. He tossed in the bag and slammed the trunk shut. "Guess we'll just have to watch it out the window. C'mon, let's eat."

There were two truckers smoking cigarettes in a booth in the corner but they didn't seem to notice us. The place smelled thick with bacon grease and it made me kind of hungry and made me kind of want to puke. A girl sat behind the counter reading newspaper comics and chewing gum. Reggie and I went to the other end of the restaurant. The girl got up and strolled over like we were just a couple of nobodies, which I guess we really were.

"What y'all want to drink?" She kept chewing her gum. She was a pretty girl even without makeup. She had a few freckles.

"Cherry Coke," Reggie said, with that big, dumb smile on his face. "And what's your name, darlin'?"

"Stacy. You know what you want to eat?" She smacked the gum in her mouth.

"Yes I do, darlin'. I'd like a T-bone steak and eggs. Over easy. You get them make the eggs nice and runny for me. You got some onions and cheese to put on 'em? And some hot sauce?"

I ordered a BLT and some water and she walked away. "Nice little piece of ass there," Reggie said. "Give me a cigarette, man." I lit one for myself as well. Reggie smoked and stared across the diner at the girl. "Maybe we should get us a room here at the motel," he said. "This'd be a good spot to lay low."

"You're fucking crazy," I said. "You think this is fun or something?"

"Kinda, man. C'mon, we're gonna be livin' large real soon. Steak and eggs, Barry. And hell, with your share—"

"So how much is my share?"

"Shit, man, I ain't even counted it yet."

"What percent?"

Reggie looked at me through the smoke. "How about twenty?"

"How about half."

"You know I did all the work," he said. "I had another buddy backed out last minute and he only said thirty. Hell, he helped me plan the whole thing."

"You never even asked me about all this."

"Shit, man, I asked you for a *ride*." Somehow Reggie made it seem like it was my fault I was in all this, and I suppose it was. Reggie was a goddamn liar and nothing was going to change that. He didn't have any friends, either. He probably stole that gun from the flea market. "I'll take forty, then. I drove the car."

"Look man, I don't want to dick around no more. I don't even know how much is in that bag."

"I want my fair share," I told him, "Or you're gonna find yourself in some serious legal shit."

"What you tryin' to say?"

"I'm saying they'll go easy on me if I turn you in."

Reggie put the cigarette down. "You listen here," he said. "We been friends a long time, Barry. But if you ever even think about goin' to the police I will blow your goddamn head clean off."

"What, with your old cowboy gun?"

Right then the girl came back with our food. Reggie's plate had a thin brown slab of meat and two bright yellow eggs. He stubbed out the cigarette and smiled at his plate like a little birthday boy. "You are sweet as pecan pie," he said to the girl, looking her up and down.

She seemed to like that, blushing a little as she walked away. Reggie picked up the steak knife and broke open one of his yolks. "Thirty-five," he said. "And that's all we're gonna talk about it. After we eat, I'll go get us a room."

THE MOTEL ROOM WAS cheap but clean, cable television, two beds, and blurry pastel pictures on the walls. The air condition-er was loud and pretty cold if you stood right by it. I took off my shirt, which was soaked through with sweat, and tossed it over the vent. Reggie claimed the bed right up next to the window and A/C. He picked up the remote control and pointed it at the television. "I wonder if they got porno on here like they do some places."

"Let's just watch the news, Reggie. They'll mention the bank no doubt. They might know it was us."

"Shit yeah, good thinkin'," he said, "let me know what they say." He went into the bathroom and I turned the volume up but it was just the weather report. Sunny and hot for the next few days, with afternoon thunderstorms. Sometimes in the summer it would rain every afternoon without cooling anything off, just turn the place into a steam bath. I was glad it hadn't rained today. My tires were near bald and I probably would've driven the car right off the road.

Reggie came back and asked for my keys. "I'll get us some beer."

"I'll go with you."

"Naw, I'm just going to run to that store we passed. You stay and watch the news, here in the cool." He had his hand out and a hangdog face. "Please, man. I'll be back in no time, swear it."

Of course I didn't trust him, but I was kind of counting on that. If he did take off, the Ventura was enough price to pay to just get away from him. I didn't care much about the money anymore. I'd have been fine taking a bus back to town, starting up on the Chevelle SS, even though I already took out the only part that was worth a damn. Or even better, maybe Reggie would get busted. Maybe he'd go down hard. "Yeah sure," I said, "here you go."

I watched the news a while. It was mostly boring stuff about some church helping out crippled kids and a city councilwoman busted for shoplifting. They recapped the robbery but just said it was two white dudes, the gunman and the driver. They also said cops thought the getaway car was green, a 90's Ford or Mercury four-door. That made me feel pretty good but also kind of sick, knowing that Reggie just might get away, and there was a pretty good chance I was never going to see my car or any of that money again.

I WOKE UP TO THE sound of gunshots and people yelling. It was some action movie on TV. The door opened up and there was Reggie with a case of Bud and a carton of cigarettes. I was surprised to see him, even more to see the girl following him. "Hey Barry, wake up," he said. "You remember Stacy, the gal that waited on us? She's come by to have a beer."

"Hey," I said.

Reggie set the groceries on the dresser. He got three cans and passed them around. He opened Stacy's for her. He looked at me. "How was the news, buddy? Anything goin' on in the world today?"

"No," I said. "Everything's just like it was before, I guess."

"See, Barry here is a news buff. He's always watchin' that shit. This guy's a real sharp guy."

"You must be pretty smart," she said, still not very interested. She wasn't chewing gum anymore. I wondered if she was old enough to be drinking beer.

Reggie flopped onto the bed, pulled a bag of weed from his pocket and rolled a joint. Stacy sat down at the table. We all sat there without saying much, listening to the explosions and Schwarzenegger grunts from the movie. Everyone had a cigarette. Stacy finally asked, "What are y'all doin' here anyway? Watchin' this movie? What is this, *The Terminator*?"

"Naw, stupid," Reggie said. "Just because that's Arnold don't make this *The Terminator*."

"Don't call her stupid, Reggie."

"C'mon, I didn't mean it."

He got up to get her another beer. She turned to me. "Don't you got any bags or clothes or anything?"

"Sure we do," Reggie said. "They're out in the car. We just ain't brought 'em in. Matter of fact, I think I'll go get our stuff." Reggie winked at me and left with the keys. Stacy and I just sat there drinking. He came back with the trash bag and threw it on the floor under the sink.

"That's y'alls clothes?" She had her thin little eyebrows cocked like she was disgusted. "Y'all keep your clothes in a garbage sack?"

"Our luggage was stolen," Reggie said. "I guess we better buy us a suitcase, huh, Barry?"

"Well it's hot in here," Stacy said, "y'all bring any swim trunks? There's a pool here and I got a suit in my bag at the diner."

"Shit yeah," said Reggie, "we don't got trunks, but we can go in our drawers, right? It's almost dark and there ain't no one around. What do you say?"

"I don't know," I said.

"We'll take the beers down there, get drunk and have a good time. Let's do this real quick, and we'll go down to the pool." He lit the joint and we all got high. We stayed there watching the movie for what felt like an hour before anybody remembered to go swimming. By then we had half a case of beer left and took it down with us.

Down by the pool we all got pretty drunk. I was content to float around on my back, listening to the sound of cicada coming and going as my ears dipped in and out of the water. Stacy wore a little blue bikini, and I remember thinking how I had no right to be so high and have her to look at. She was real skinny but pretty, the way her blonde hair got slicked back and dark when it was wet. She probably saw me looking at her; she smiled and dove under the water. She swam like a bluegill.

Reggie was in the water next to me, resting against the wall of the shallow end with his arms spread over the edge. He clicked his tongue and watched her too. "You ain't getting no percentage of that," he said. Stacy popped out of the water next to the beers and Reggie whistled at her. She grabbed three more and waded through the water back to us.

"What are you boys doin' out here in the middle of nowhere?"

Reggie just chuckled, stoned and drunk and his eyes poring over her body.

"We told you. We're just on a little road trip."

"Where y'all goin', then?"

"Shit, we're just goin' down the road." Reggie skimmed his hand in an arc across the surface of the water.

"Y'all just packed up and left without any plans or anything?"

"Didn't even pack up," he said. "What about you, girlie? You do anything besides sling fried eggs and patty melts?"

"I'm on summer break. I'm in nursing school."

Reggie clicked his tongue one more time. "I bet you'd be real fine in one of them nurse's outfits."

She grinned and then looked away, maybe at the sky, but somewhere past us, anyway. "I wish I could just pack up and leave like that." She looked like some kind of starlet.

Reggie paid no attention. "Girl, I could play doctor with you all night."

I floated off when Reggie started to chase her around the shallow end. She was laughing and squealing and carrying on, then she got out of the pool and said she was going back to the room. Reggie told me if I wanted to I could wait ten minutes and come up to watch if I was quiet. I didn't say a word back to him.

"Well," he said, "just remember to bring the beer when you come back up."

T HAT MORNING HIT ME pretty hard. I woke up having to piss and the little crack of light between the curtains hit right in my eyes. Reggie and Stacy were still asleep, all of them covered up under the sheets, which was kind of a mixed blessing. I watched the two of them there and thought about what I was going to do that day, what was next. I wondered how long I would have to put up with this dirtbag. Reggie was nice, I guess, but he was a plain loser, unshaven and disgusting, and I wondered how he could ever pull off a bank robbery and wind up eating steak for breakfast and sleeping with a hotass girl. He was a loser all right, but he had pulled it off and he had got the girl, which meant he had something I didn't.

I looked over at the bag full of money, all lumpy there on the floor next to the sink. I thought of taking it and taking off, but Reggie had proven himself a psycho and he knew where my mother and I live. I looked at the money sitting there and I thought—Reggie is exactly the kind of guy who would keep his clothes in a garbage sack.

I rolled out of bed, walked on my tiptoes around the room gathering up my shirt and shoes. I still needed my car keys, which were still in Reggie's jeans. I crept over real slow and quiet to where the two of them were just a lump of covers and muffled snoring. I picked up his pants and Stacy stirred a little under the sheets, mumbled something and came to rest again. Then I figured, what the hell. I picked Reggie's jeans up off the floor and left the room with them in my hand.

I kind of hated stealing a man's pants away from him, but I figured he could afford another pair now. It was the only thing I could do to him anyway. He had the girl after all, and he could just tell her he robbed a bank and she'd probably fall in love with him, and they'd buy another car and hit the road together and have sex all across the country.

It was warm and humid. From the balcony I saw the sun poke through the trees and I knew it was going to be another hot day. I almost wanted to get back in the pool. I put on my shoes outside the door and went around the building to piss in the bushes. I took my keys out of his pocket and left his jeans there by the building, but not right in the piss, because that would just be wrong.

It was only about fifty miles back to town. I was still sleepy and kind of dizzy and needing a cup of coffee and a donut. I ran into the diner and bought one from a much older woman working the counter who was ugly and wore too much makeup.

In the car I cranked up the engine and it made a low rumbling sound that sounded good even if it was loud enough to hear from the room. I gripped the wheel, glad to be in the driver's seat and headed home. I looked in the rearview mirror to back out but nearly jumped through the windshield and spilled my coffee all over the place. She was in the backseat, smiling at me.

"Is your name really Barry?" Stacy said.

"What the hell are you doin' in my car?"

"Reggie told me what y'all did."

"Motherfuck."

"A bag of money don't look nothin' like a bag of clothes, hun." She put her hand on the sack next to her on the seat. Her bikini was draped over it and it all looked sexy and beautiful.

"That son of a bitch in there is real dumb, isn't he?" she asked, still grinning. "I don't know about you, though. First I thought, why would he just walk away from all this cash? But it ain't because you're dumb. It's because you're a good person. And I kind of like that about you."

I just sat there. I probably looked pretty stupid.

"I knew you were gonna leave. I could tell that. That Reggie's an idiot. We should get out of here together. We could go down to Tunica and get a room, have a real nice time. There's a ton of cash here."

She was right, there was a ton of cash and her right next to it—right in my backseat was everything that I could've ever asked for and slim chance that I'd have to own up for any of it. I thought that maybe I deserved this, that the situation had straightened out and I was finally given what Reggie never deserved in all his life. It was like I had robbed that bank, and now I was offered the girl and the money and the chance to get away with it. And it was all right there waiting for me to say yes, but I still knew I'd never have the balls to take it.

"You were right about me," I said. "I'm a good person. I just want to go home."

She got a little pouty then, very sexy, but only for a second.

"Then get the fuck out of the car," she said. I heard a little noise come from the seat behind me, sounded just like Reggie's tongue clicked against his teeth, but I was sure it wasn't.

the BULL interview:

CHUCK KLOSTERMAN

Chuck Klosterman has established himself as the patron saint of American popular culture and contrarianism. He is currently a Consulting Editor on the website Grantland.com and has written for Spin, Esquire, GQ, *and* The New York Times *Magazine. His nonfiction books—*Fargo Rock City, Sex, Drugs, and Cocoa Puffs, Killing Yourself to Live, Chuck Klosterman IV, *and* Eating the Dinosaur—*have explored virtually every nook and cranny of our common experiences and guilty pleasures. With* Downtown Owl *in 2008 and* The Visible Man *released last fall, he's ventured into the world of novels. Here are his thoughts on writing, the future of publishing, critics of his work, and the possibility of it all falling apart.*

—*Jared Yates Sexton*

JYS: Why fiction? I mean, I feel like you've built up your name with essays and you're well known as a pop culture philosopher. You've established yourself in that way; why go this route?

CK: I guess there are probably several answers to this. I feel like if I would've started with fiction and then wrote nonfiction the question would be flipped. To me it isn't that weird to do both. It's definitely easier to publish your first book by going the nonfiction route. That's definitely true. I'd been considering the things I wrote about in my first book for ten years, so that was very obviously what I was going to write. I then wrote *Sex, Drugs, and Cocoa Puffs*, which seemed to me to be a natural extension because I was thinking of things the same way, only it wasn't related to metal. Those two books seem pretty similar, both in how they're written and how you will probably like one if you like the other. Then I wrote *Killing Yourself to Live*, which is structured like a novel I guess, except that it actually happened. And it has a weird ending because, well, life is weird. At that point I knew I wanted to try and write fiction. I guess I always wanted to. I mean, the novel is the hardest thing to write. You start and you're staring at empty white space on your computer. Every little thing you're creating is yours; you're creating your own reality.

The other thing I'd like to say is that nonfiction way outsells fiction. My other books will definitely way, way, way outsell *The Visible Man*, which will only sell a fraction of what my other books do. But that's not why I'm doing it. If I wanted to be as successful as possible I just would've kept writing *Sex, Drugs, and Cocoa Puffs* over and over again. I would've had a similar title, a similar structure, just because you know that that works. But that's not how I look at it. I do what I'm interested in doing. You can't do X because X is what other people seem to like the most.

JYS: I understand you could've gone that route, but I was wondering—when you were younger, when you were cutting your teeth on writing, did you have ideas, novels even, that you abandoned? Have you been writing stories? I feel like when *Decade* came out with the long fictional section at the end it was jarring. I remember having conversations with people who were wondering what the hell you were doing.

CK: Well, I can tell you what I was doing. It makes a lot of sense, even though I'm a little ashamed to admit it. What happened was that I was on the *Killing Yourself to Live* Tour and I was talking to bigger audiences, and a lot of young people would come up and say they had no idea I was a journalist. Is there anywhere we can read your articles? And I was excited that they'd want to read my articles. So I wanted to do this thing where I'd print an anthology of my work, and I'd print it in soft-cover, and it will really just be for college kids. I told Scribner about this and they thought it'd be a great idea, but we should publish it in hardcover too because you only make a profit when you publish in hardcover. So I was like, okay, we'll do that. And then, when it came out, I don't know if you remember this, but it had a complicated slipcover on it? Well, that was extremely expensive to do, so the book was going to be even more expensive than anything I'd done before. On top of that, I knew that most of the people who were going to buy this book were going to like my writing, and maybe a lot of them had already read the articles that were going to be in there.

So I said, you know what I'm going to do? I've been working on a novel in Akron and I gave up on it, so I'm going to include that because I know no one had read that. I put a novella in that was supposed to be the beginning of a novel. It was all mapped out in my mind. It was that guy who has the woman land on his car, and he's going to find out this happened to someone in Colorado, and then he realizes there's this whole cult of people who are disenfranchised with life and the only thing they can do is take a bunch of drugs, fly an airplane, jump out while having sex, and then die. That just didn't work out—it didn't seem good to me.

But I had this beginning to this book and I put it in *Decade*, but maybe I shouldn't have. Most people who comment on that story say that they think it's bad. Even my wife told me it's a bad story. I didn't think anybody would care. I just thought that people would be happier getting something extra rather than getting something less.

JYS: How many novels have you tried?

CK: Well, I seriously tried to write four—two I completed and two I stopped. The second one I stopped was the one from *Decade* and the first was back when I was living in Fargo and I think it was about a girl?

JYS: So, do you have aspirations? I know that's a strange question, but do you feel like you were just doing something you wanted to do or were you trying to be a great fiction writer? I noticed in *Downtown Owl* and *The Visible Man* that you make a lot of allusions to great writers and great works—do you have an interest in being known like that?

CK: I will admit it's not that I aspire to be a great novelist, but I was extremely worried that my first novel (*Downtown Owl*) was going to be terrible. That was my big concern because it would then be this realization that I could only do this one thing, that being semi-autobiographical criticism. So my aspiration was to write something acceptable that someone would read and wouldn't think it was awful. I'm sure some people think it's awful, but for the most part it seems to have worked out.

The other aspiration I have comes from the fact that I don't like a lot of novels. I just don't. I find that even novels that are often perceived as great, or recognized as great, are not fun to read. I lose interest and they seem fake to me. So I thought to myself that I'd like to write novels in a way that I'd like to read them. The way that they would be structured, the way the characters talked, and obviously I do one thing that's the opposite of what people always say to do—that being "show, don't tell." I think that's better advice visually, for a film, but in a book sometimes it's better just to say this is the idea and deal with it that way. That's sort of what I aspire to when I write these—I want to write books that I wish I would've stumbled across and read.

JYS: Well then, hypothetically, because I know you like hypotheticals, let's say that *The Visible Man* came out and there's some kind of crazy attention heaped on it. All of a sudden it's considered a book that changes American culture and revives the idea of the Great American Novel. How would you feel about your identity as a writer? Because I think most people know you as a pop culture or nonfiction writer, so how would you feel if all of a sudden you were seen as Chuck Klosterman, Novelist?

CK: Okay. The simple answer is that I'd think it was great. *(laughs)* That would be awesome if that happened. The longer answer is that I would intuitively know it was fake. I would know that what was happening would not be a product of the work, but more so the product of culture deciding it could be used for those purposes. I mean, I know it would be partially based on the work, but, you know, when something like that happens to anybody it's not all accurate. If you remember Dave Eggers first book (*A Heartbreaking Work of Staggering Genius*) was the center of most conversations about culture, or *Freedom* (by Jonathan Franzen). Those are both great books by great writers. They're well done and well executed. But their movement into import, and sort of the evolution of those books, is sort of a fake thing we've agreed to do. So with my book, if that happened, I would think to myself, it's really funny that this book about how the world is fake is trying to explain its own success.

JYS: Isn't that worldview troubling as a writer or a cultural personality? If that's the case, then aren't all books and movies and songs that are important are so based upon arbitrary decisions? So then, at the end of the day, is that how you explain your success?

CK: Not really, no, because we're talking about different things here. There's a difference between a thing's value and its perceived value. If the Beatles had not become successful somehow, if culture was not ready for rock music until the 70's or something like that, and the Beatles made music but are sort of a little footnote to history, those songs would be just as moving and incredible. But because we have a collective understanding of their value, there are two experiences with their music—one is where their music comes out of the speakers, and two is your actual concept.

I mean, I tried to write the best book I could, to the best of my ability, and like all writers I have certain limitations. There are things I'm good at, things I'm not good at, and I'm trying to figure those out. In the middle of that, I'm trying to write the best book I can. However, I'm very aware that the success of the book, and the quality of the book, are only partially connected. *Sex, Drugs, and Cocoa Puffs* is not the best book I've done. I kind of think it's the worst one. But that's not how it's consumed by people. It's by far the best to them. So I'm not sure if my un-recognition of the reality of the world necessarily changes how I would write anything.

JYS: How do you feel about *The Visible Man* then? Do you feel like you hit your mark? How does it compare with *Downtown Owl* for instance?

CK: *Downtown Owl* was more personal, I guess, because I sort of felt like I was the only person in a position to write that book and have it be read. It was rural North Dakota, pre-Internet—that book's not going to happen if I didn't write it, and I didn't want that time and place to be lost. Even if it's bad, I thought, it'll come out. Because those were my motives, it probably will always seem pretty personal, because it is. It's one aspect of a perceived reality. This book (*The Visible Man*) is different because it's an idea book that's built around the premise that you don't have to like the characters. I liked this concept of a partially invisible person trying to understand the authentic parts of the world. And I wondered what type of person would be smart enough and motivated enough to do it? It would be a really bad, egocentric person who would sort of have a warped view about what was important about being alive. And I thought, okay, what kind of therapist would not only listen to him lecture, but sort of become charmed by his madness? All right, someone who was insecure and intelligent, but not necessarily smart.

Since there are only two characters that people can try and care about—and might not—I can imagine someone reading this book and saying that they came away without caring about anybody in it. So that was obviously a problem, but that's how it had to be. How do I feel about it? I think I've felt better about the last two books I've written (*The Visible Man* and *Eating the Dinosaur*) than any of the others. I guess maybe it's because I'm older and maybe a little less nervous in general.

JYS: I noticed that those books have a real underlying theme of reality versus perceived reality. Were you working on that idea and that's what led to the creation of *The Visible Man* character, or did you have him and he lent himself to that theme?

CK: I think you get into periods of your life where certain questions seem more important than others. When I first got into writing books, I kind of thought the important thing was this gap between the experience audiences had with culture and how it was represented in the media. That was really important to me. Then, in the middle of the books, I've gotten more interested in my own life and less interested in how other people experience things. And now, I guess it really started before *Eating the Dinosaur*, because it and *The Visible Man* have a lot of similar themes in a weird way, I just kind of came to this conclusion that this was the central question of our time period—what is reality? You could say that question's been asked forever and has been reconciled in the past and that only stoners talk about it now. But I think that particularly the change in technology and the proliferation of media in ways that are both sort of predictable, but also unprecedented—we didn't know what would happen with twenty-four hour news and things like that. You read old science fiction and there are things happening that were like the Internet, but it was never considered that this was something ordinary people would be grappling with. Meaning, people have to wonder now who they are, who they are on Twitter or Facebook, and what is that relationship? To me it seems to be the most important thing. The writers I'm most interested in right now, like Jonathan Lethem, these are elements in their books. A lot of these books that are singing to me now are these people thinking about the same problem.

So I did that book of essays (*Eating the Dinosaur*) and then I did the novel which allowed me to have characters say the things I wanted to say without them being directly tied to me. That was part of the thing with *Downtown Owl* too. For years there I was a journalist and I was writing about the world through other people's quotes. So many times I found myself thinking, I wish they'd just say this, this thing that I'm thinking about, and what is actually what they're trying to say through their collection of words. They're not able to because it's not exactly clear to them and thoughts are confusing. So I wanted to write a book where I could have people say what I'd always wanted them to say.

JYS: Is that the appeal of fiction? You brought up an interesting idea of how culture has changed reality. The things we consider the most real—reality shows, celebrity culture, the twenty-four hour news cycle—and the things we pay most attention to for defining reality are fictional pieces. They're books and movies and television shows, right?

CK: That's a good question and I think you're right on. As for novels and visual media, I agree that it does seem that shows like *The Wire*, *Breaking Bad*, *Mad Men* have replaced novels in a culture. I don't mean that in a negative way, it's just that we're dealing with things and problems through this medium in the same way we have novels. It's not even depressing to me that this is happening. If you really think about it objectively, a story with a visual component that you can have a relationship with is just more pleasant. You can't really go back once you've had a story told to you via multiple views.

JYS: About the relationship between novels and shows as deliverers of fiction and reality, I've found that a lot more writers try and write stories and novels, but also dip their feet in that other well. They have that idea for a dramatic series in their back pocket. It's alluring because you have the literary aspect and the aesthetics of a visual product. Do you have any desire to get into that business?

CK: It would be great to do that. It would be so fun to make a show like *Mad Men*, but here's the deal—it's not a self-contained enterprise. The appeal of writing a novel is that I can really do it by myself. Of all the qualities of writing, that's probably the thing I like the most. I, alone, can create any reality where I want to work in. If I made a television series, that would require not only the writing, but the pitching of the show, the handing over of the process to someone else, because I don't know how to fucking make a TV show. I could be involved in the process, but I don't know how to use a camera or build a set. And then there's the casting where people are going to become the people you imagined, whether they fit what you imagined in the first place or not. And they're going to become those characters, whether you like it or not. It's a collaborative thing and I don't know how much I would like that.

JYS: You have your fingers in lot of pies already, though. It seems like you're everywhere, so I'm curious about your actual writing process. What's it like on a day-to-day basis and what it's like on a larger, idea-creation scale?

CK: When I wrote *The Visible Man* there was a time where I decided that this was the main focus and everything else was secondary. I rented an office outside of my house and I would go there at noon and would screw around on the Internet for an hour and then write from one to five. I'd just try and make sure that I always wrote a thousand words. If I didn't do that, I'd make myself think about something in a different way so that the next day I'd start over without being in the same spot. But I don't have a process the way other writers do. It doesn't seem like it when I talk to other authors. They have a lot of rituals. They write at certain times. There are certain things they listen to. I get an idea and I think about it until I have an open stretch of time and then I write it out. That's as far as it goes. I guess, in a way I write fast. But in another, I write slow. Does only the typing count? Then I can write a column for Grantland in two hours. But I thought about the thing for four days. So did it take me four days, or two hours? I don't know what counts. I don't know if all writers are like this. I'm thinking about things all the time. Whether I'm at the gym, watching TV, or writing other people's books. All the time. So when I do sit down it's basically just about the typing.

JYS: But you seem to have your fingers on the pulse of a lot of things. How does your day fill up?

CK: Hmm. I think the one thing that people seem to think about me is that I am consciously pursuing this study of popular culture to write about. They'll ask me about *Grey's Anatomy*, because it's so popular, and they'll expect me to think something about it, but I've never watched it. I only follow the things that I'm actively interested in. I just feel like the organic process of consuming culture is kind of at the core of what we do. I'm not trying to trick myself into watching or liking something because if I comment on it, I'm going to be coming from the perspective of someone who doesn't like it to begin with. It's like work to me.

I get up and I listen to music, whatever I feel like listening to, and I read news and talk to a lot of my friends, who are really smart, and whatever they're talking about, bands or authors or movies they've seen, these are things that are not just good, but meaningful. They wouldn't mention them if they weren't. So I feel naturally plugged into that stuff. My wife gets home from work and we usually watch movies or television. It was different when I was single because everything was built around writing. I liked to write then from eleven at night to four in the morning. A lot of my life was structured around this weird window of time where I did my work. Now I live a much more normal life and have to find time to write during the day.

JYS: I think it's a weird mystery, the process of writing, and I always find it strange when a writer tells me they write at this certain time of day, while eating this sandwich, or whatever. It feels put on.

CK: It seems that way to me too. But it might have something to do with backgrounds. Working in newspapers for eight years does change your process. Probably improves it. The process becomes— this happened. Write about it. It's really acting in the present tense and you're often writing about things you don't know anything about, and you're trying to become a near expert as quickly as possible. And all through college, a lot of my life I guess, I thought I'd write a book at some point. I thought I'd always work in newspapers because I thought newspapers would always be around. So I guess I have the mentality of a newspaper writer, even though I don't really write like one. And I probably didn't write like one when I was at a paper and at the time it was a problem. Now it's probably a benefit.

JYS: I think when a writer gains confidence in what they're doing that's probably when they start getting really good, when they stop worrying about it. Do you ever read criticism of your work?

CK: I read all of it. It's always interesting. I don't believe it though. The person is usually either saying you're way better than you are, or way worse. The compliments they give you are totally fake and the criticisms are all of these things that they're working out about themselves or the things they'd like to see in the actual world. I've been a critic my whole life and I know how this is. I know that criticism is autobiography and anyone who says it isn't is lying. Even if they've convinced themselves. If they were being as objective and outside of themselves as possible—they'd never use "I" in a review or anything like that—it's still their mind they're using to interpret.

So I'm always interested in what people are writing about me, but it's all unreal. The negative things always seem more true, that's just human nature. I mean, if you get one bad review and fourteen positive ones, you're always going to remember the bad one. That's your own type of insecurity. For me, I know these reviews are going to exist whether I read them or not, so I might as well read them. I've spent my whole life thinking about other forms of art. When I was in eighth grade, I was interested in what magazines were writing about the new W.A.S.P. album. Of course, when people started writing about my work, it was really weird and exciting and uncomfortable. All of these things. I just want to see what they say.

JYS: Are you ever anxious about it?

CK: To be honest, my biggest fear is that all of this is just going to end one day. It started so seemingly arbitrarily. In 1999 nobody cared what I said about anything. I was working at the Akron Beacon Journal and nobody fucking gave a shit in Akron. No one cared. And all of a sudden, these things changed. And not only did they care, they cared too much, which was the weirdest part of all of it. That was odd, but I have this great life now. It's so much better than I ever thought it'd be. And of course I complain about it—I'm kind of a pessimistic person—but the actual conditions of my life are so much greater than I could have ever believed that I'm just waiting on it to stop. Things changed so much the first time that I know they can change back. So I think, what if *The Visible Man* sells four thousand copies? And nobody cares? And if they don't care about this one they won't care about the next one. And if someone comes around and fills the hole in culture that I fill, and there are no papers to go back to, and maybe I'd just be writing these books out of some kind of reflexive reaction to not knowing what else to do.

JYS: What happens if it all comes crumbling down? Are you going to be on VH1 in a stupor, talking about the good ol' days?

CK: Well, I don't spend any of my money, so I'd be okay there. I would keep writing because I like writing. I never trust my sense of myself, meaning I feel really weird sometimes about the way my writing is perceived or how I'm perceived. It's weird when strangers talk about you. It feels bad sometimes. But I think sometimes, would it be worse if it didn't happen? Do I actually, unknowingly, crave this? It doesn't seem that way to me, but how would I really know? I see other people and see how often they're unable to understand integral things about their personality that other people are able to see easily. They're missing the most obvious, clearest thing about themselves. So, I wonder, am I like that? Is there something that everybody else knows about me and am I the only one who doesn't? As I'm saying this to you right now, I wonder in my mind, does this guy know a truth about me that is so obvious that he's actually stopping himself from laughing?

THE MOON'S FACE, DARKENED

Kevin Wilson

MY WIFE WAS LEAVING me with her brother, who had just left his wife, so she could camp out with her wilderness skills club in order to view a total lunar eclipse. "It's a tradition," Carrie said when I asked why I couldn't come with her, why I had to stay with Morgan, her drunk, dickhead of a brother who was sixteen years older than her and therefore more like an uncle. A drunk, dickhead of an uncle.

"We've been getting together since high school for each total lunar eclipse," she said, wearing a knit cap that had been stitched with the word *Lunartic*. "We haven't had one in almost three years."

She talked about things like tradition and catching up with old friends but I understood that the real reason was that she was going to sleep with some outdoorsy type who had complicated knots displayed on the walls of his study, that she had been sleeping with this guy since high school, and I was not to deprive her of this.

Morgan, her brother, sat on the couch sipping rum and coke through a straw and asked what was so special about a lunar eclipse.

"Nothing," my wife said, "but a total lunar eclipse is very special."

She told him the story that I had heard dozens of times, how Columbus—his crew having robbed and murdered some of the welcoming natives—saved his own life by using an astronomical almanac to correctly predict a total eclipse of the moon, inflamed with wrath, in order to scare the chief. "Shee-it," Morgan said, making a wanking motion with his hand, "I wouldn't have fallen for that science bullshit. I would have killed Columbus with my bare hands and then my tribe would have thought I was some kind of heap big badass."

"Then his crew would have shot you right in the ass with their rifles," I said.

"Not so fast, Poindexter," he said. "I'd turn sideways, cut their target in half. They wouldn't hit jack shit with those popguns."

"Can I leave?" my wife asked.

"Go on," Morgan said.

"Please don't go," I said.

"Bye," my wife said, and she was gone.

I asked Morgan if he knew any of the people in my wife's club.

"A couple," he said.

"Does Carrie want to fuck any of them?" I asked.

He shrugged his shoulders. "Could be," he said. "She likes mountain men."

"I'm not a mountain man," I said.

"No," he admitted. "As far as I've seen, you're not really the outdoor type."

THAT NIGHT, DRUNK ON bourbon and Sun Drop, Morgan took out a very mini-Casio keyboard, almost the size of a credit card, and turned on the rhumba beat. He began to play "Unchained Melody" slurring the words "to the open arms of the sea" so that it sounded like "tootie hope and harms odyssey."

I watched the World Submission Fighting Finals on ESPN, two Brazilians wrapping themselves around and around each other, trying very hard, I thought, not to accidentally fuck.

"Jimmy's fat," Morgan then sang, punching the keys of the Casio with great emphasis. "He's got two cheeseburgers and a super-sized Coke... Jimmy's fat." This was to the tune of Beck's "Where It's At". I turned off the grappling in mid-heel-hook and faced my brother-in-law, his mouth turned into a cartoon-styled frown.

"What are you doing?" I asked.

"I just wrote this," he said, still playing, the Casio set to Funk. "You know Jimmy Patrick?" he asked. Jimmy Patrick had been a classmate of Morgan's and had killed himself a few months ago.

"Not really," I said.

"He was a fat motherfucker," Morgan said. "I hated him so much."

"I thought you were friends," I said.

"We were kind of friends," Morgan said, sounding the same note over and over, staring off into space.

"He killed himself," I said.

"Shit, I know that," Morgan said.

"Well, I didn't really know him," I said, and turned the TV back on to the next match, some fat-ass Russian and another arm-breaker from Brazil.

"Fifth grade," Morgan said, "Jimmy stood up to do a problem at the blackboard and when he sat back down, I set up a pencil under him and it went straight up his rectum."

I turned away from the TV. "What now?" I said.

"I sent a pencil up his butt," Morgan said, about to cry.

"What now?"

"Jimmy squeaked and the teacher asked what was the matter,

but he wouldn't say. He just looked down at his desk and wouldn't move."

"You say you put a pencil up Jimmy Patrick's butt?" I said, and Morgan nodded.

"You set up a pencil and it managed to puncture the fabric of his pants, the fabric of his underwear, and just so happened to be perfectly aligned with his asshole?" I said, and Morgan again nodded.

"I'm having a hard time believing that, Morgan."

"Right up his butt," he said.

"Fine," I said. "Okay."

On the TV, the Russian was putting some kind of anaconda choke on the Brazilian, who kept rolling over, which only cinched the choke tighter. I was positive—as positive as I was that my wife was fucking some guy under the shadow of a blood-red moon—that Morgan and Jimmy had engaged in some weird sex stuff when they were teenagers and it had probably led to Jimmy killing himself and Morgan subsequently leaving his wife. Morgan played the opening part of "Lean on Me" and then gently set the keyboard on the table. Ten minutes later, he was dead asleep.

I went outside and stared up at the moon, angry and rusted, ruined. I wished I lived in a time when I could point to the sky, at the oddness occurring for only a brief time, and wield some kind of power over those who had no idea how the world worked.

GOTHICCEY AND BECKETTEY

Padgett Powell

Y OU CAN'T GO THROUGH life shaking hands with chickens. Momma said chickens don't last long enough to hold up their end of the bargain. Daddy said let's get some whiskey and quick grits. Momma said Daddy fell out one night in a ditch and they found a dead water moccasin under him the next day. Daddy said he meant no harm to that snake nortany other he just won't some whiskey and grits. Momma said who did I marry. Daddy said whigrits. Momma said chickens are dufi. Dedsaid how you know latin. Msaid shutafuckup. Dedwhupper side the head broom handle. I said I better get out o here. Deysaid youright bout thetboy, get a fuck outta here afore we rescind your license to be progeny the fruit of our vigorous and juicy loins. Momsed Diddy when you talk like at I get even mojuicy Diddysaid I heard that Jellyroll git down in the servile position I will toss you one.

SEP AR A TION

Tom Bonfiglio

THE WEEKEND IS GRAVID with promise for Jon Porter, two days without a tie, without calculating risk and adjusting rates, two whole days of fucking Jill, playing board games and watching TV, maybe a little yard work thrown in for productivity's sake. He can strip and paint that dresser in the spare bedroom. They'll smoke pot and swim naked. The air practically shimmers.

She's waiting for him in the bedroom, Jill, freshly showered and no doubt naked under a crisp white sheet, her tan skin, her black hair still wet and somewhat tangled, leaving a shadow of water on the pillowcase. There hasn't been a single moment in his life when he was not in love with her; not one second. They're good together. They match. Just the two of them. They don't need anybody else. The bong on the night table is filled and waiting.

Yet before he can get his tie off, before he can even weigh the option of jumping into bed right now or taking a rip off the bong first, the doorbell rings. It takes a moment before either of them recognizes the sound, they hear it so infrequently. Nobody visits them. They are private people.

"Should we ignore it?" Jill whispers, as if the person outside is listening.

"They'll go away," Jon says, grabbing the bong and lighting the bowl.

The bell rings again and Jill rises, the sheet falling off of her, and a breeze from the ceiling fan perking the nipples on her small-ish breasts. "Just get it," she says. "I'll come out if it's anything."

The bell rings twice again before Jon reaches the door, where his neighbor, Gayle, through the peephole looks like a severed head trapped in a fishbowl. Gayle is a small, wiry mutt of a woman who speed-walks around the neighborhood always in some sort of huff. On his porch, she carries a clipboard and pen.

"There's something I need to sit down and talk to you about," Gayle says. "The both of you."

Her concern worries him, the way it advertises itself on her face in worry lines so deep they could hold a penny. Concern of that intensity is something he's made a point to run away from his entire life. Her insistent voice too, and how it makes even a hello in the supermarket feel like a lecture—he knew that tone all too well as a teenager, in talks with his parents, his aunts and uncles. Since then he's done his best to avoid people like her, and his family as well, immediate and extended.

"Okay," he says. And for the first time ever, the Porters have a visitor.

Their living room is brightly decorated, canary yellow walls and furniture made of red and blue leather, a fireplace looking through to the kitchen and wrapped in shiny stainless steel. Gayle takes one couch and thank god Jill arrives, in a pair of shorts and T-shirt, barefoot and braless and leading him to the other couch where they sit together and face their neighbor.

As wiry and small as she is, Gayle sure has massive hands. They remind him of his mother's hands, and he's sure it would hurt if she were to slap him. It's a habit of his, seeing a woman's hands and estimating how hard a slap would feel, how long it would leave his face red. Gayle's hands make him flinch.

She hands Jill some papers held together by a paper clip. A man's mugshot covers the first page, though nothing seems terribly criminal about his bland, pleasant face. He looks like he could be anybody's favorite cousin. The documents peg him as Fred Bryce and the name resonates somehow, until Jon can place the man three doors down, moved in a month ago with a youngish and very pretty wife. According to the sheet, Fred Bryce is a convicted felon, a sex offender. Four years in prison for lewd and lascivious behavior with a minor. Thirteen years old. Bryce is smiling in the mug shot—looks pretty satisfied for a guy under arrest, Porter thinks. They must have taken the picture before he knew what his sentence was. Or right after he did whatever it was he did.

"What does this have to do with us?" Jill says.

Attached to Gayle's clipboard there is a petition with several pages curled over the top, already filled with the names and addresses of his neighbors listed one after another.

"I want him out of here," says Gayle. "I have daughters. I don't want this rapist around my daughters. There's a lot of us with children in this neighborhood and we all feel the same way."

"I'm sorry," Jon says, "but I'm not signing something that says a man doesn't have a right to live in his own house."

"And it doesn't say anything here about rape," Jill says.

"That's what it means. He raped a thirteen year old girl."

"It could be a boy," Jon offers. "It might have been a boy."

"It was a girl," she says. "I happen to know it was a girl though her name is private. Otherwise I'd get her involved in this too."

"Is it possible he was framed?" Jon says.

"He pleaded guilty," Gayle says, rubbing her eyes under her glasses. "Those of us with children can't sleep at night. We need him out of here. Every family in the subdivision, men, women, and children over fourteen, they've all signed. Except for you two."

"You're telling me that Fred Bryce and his wife signed a petition saying he's not welcome in his own house?"

Jill laughs. "I'm sorry," she says, "but that was funny."

Gayle's mouth has dropped open, so wide Jon can count five fillings—four silver, one black. "A child being raped is funny?" she says. "I don't understand. Explain to me what part of that is funny."

"It's not funny," Jon says. "But he owns his house. He did his time and according to the state or county or whatever he's paid his dues and rehabilitated."

"But we need to be unanimous," Gayle says.

"You really think signing a piece of paper will get him to move?"

"It's symbolic."

"So you want to shit all over this man's life but you want to do it symbolically."

Gayle scoffs. She sighs and leans forward, holding her hands like some politician. "What if he did this to someone you love?" she says. "Could you live with that? Maybe not a daughter, but what about your mother? Or a sister?"

She looks at him as if waiting for an actual answer to her question. When nothing comes, she shakes her head with something like pity, and Jill squeezes his hand so tight it almost hurts. "If you two only had children," Gayle says. "Then you'd understand."

"Get out of my house," Jill says. "Now." She stands and practically lifts Gayle off the couch and shoves her out the door, taking her clipboard with all the signatures and throwing it into the street. The metal clip sends off small yellow sparks.

Later that night Jon grows so excited that after fucking Jill twice he still has enough energy to masturbate while she poses on all fours and though he expects just a sad, watery dribble he's surprised to shoot so hard it misses her back entirely and hits the shade of his reading lamp where it drips like wax from a hot white candle.

THE NEXT MORNING THE doorbell wakes them up.

"Oh my God," Jon says. "This is getting out of control."

Jill sweats when she sleeps and her black hair has stuck to her face and forehead. She pulls the retainer out of her mouth and yawns. "I really hope that guy isn't a rapist," she says. "It'd be nice to have another couple without kids."

"I'm not one to judge him," he says, stepping into the nearest pair of shorts. "I know what you looked like when you were thirteen." He kisses her warm, sour mouth and the bell rings again.

Downstairs it's Claude, the pool man. Claude never comes to the door, but slips in and out the back every Saturday morning while they sleep, skimming and cleaning and shocking the pool and sending his bills through the mail. Every year at Christmas he leaves a card taped to the door, a photo of him dressed in a red velvet suit cleaning a pool, signed Santa Claude. Jon wouldn't even know who he is otherwise.

"I've got some bad news for you," Claude says. "Really bad news."

"How much will it cost?"

"No, nothing like that. The pool's okay, but you'll have to start doing it yourself. I'm sorry, Jon, but that bitch has me over a barrel."

Gayle has given him an ultimatum—either stop cleaning the Porter's pool or lose every last customer in the subdivision. "She told me the same thing about the rapist's pool," he says. "I started cleaning his too and she read me the riot act. These people will do what she says. All she has to do is snap her fingers and I'll be out of a job."

"He didn't rape anybody. She's making that up."

"I'm sorry, Jon, really. There's nothing I can do. You'll probably have to find a new landscaper to cut your grass, too."

According to the phone book, there's a pool supply store right next to the supermarket. He'd never noticed it there before, never even considered that a single store might exist dedicated to selling only pool supplies. The closest he'd ever come to understanding the maintenance of a pool was writing Claude's name on a check every month.

That afternoon Jon walks up and down the aisles, dumbstruck by how many choices there are. Nine different kinds of skimmers. Does he need powdered chlorine or these enormous Pez-shaped tabs? What about Ph? Hydrochloric acid? He could hire a new pool man but figures if that idiot Santa Claude can do it so can he. He drives home three hundred dollars poorer with a trunk full of chemicals and a skimmer pole sticking out his side window.

Jill's not in the house when he gets home. And when he looks out the kitchen window it's a surprise to see Fred Bryce, the Fred Bryce of rapist fame, standing at the edge of Jon's pool in a pair of bright yellow swim trunks, holding his own long blue pool skimmer and running it through the water like a gondolier. The hair on his chest is red and he wears a thin gold chain around his neck. Jill is sitting on the diving board in her black bikini and for a second Jon feels a spark of panic, until he sees Bryce's blonde wife also out there, face down on one of their chaise-lounges and the clasp unhooked on her lime-green top. He is amazed, and shocked, and feeling somewhat betrayed. Jon doesn't believe in making friends, and until now neither did Jill. It was something of a pact between them: keep everybody else out, the two of them a singular unit, battle-worn and time-tested. He finds his sunglasses and pastes on a smile.

"They insisted," Jill calls from the diving board. "I couldn't stop them."

"You don't have to do this," he tells Bryce. "I appreciate it, but you don't have to do this."

"Fred Bryce," he says, pumping his hand, "but I guess you know that already." He looks soft, obviously not part of the weightlifting crowd in prison. His face is pink and bland and seems twenty years older than it looked in that mugshot, though it was taken only seven years ago.

"Let me get this out straight off the bat," he says. "Anybody on that bitch's shitlist—and excuse my language but she is a bitch—is okay by me. I tried to explain my situation, our situation, to her. She wouldn't listen."

"It was me," chirps Bryce's wife. "I was the so-called victim. I'm the one he went to jail over." She reaches around and closes her bikini strap before sitting up. "I'm Kim," she says, lifting a hand to Jon. Her eyes are the same blue as the pool tiles, and her hair as blonde as can be without being white.

"We're married. She's my wife now, lawful and all that. When we met, I was eighteen and she was thirteen. It was love, though, plain and simple. She was a kid but I was too, y'know? And thirteen isn't always a child. Hell, in Shakespeare's time, and ancient history and all that—"

"We never even did it," Kim says. The expression makes her sound as young as she looks—twenty, twenty-one tops. "Not until I was eighteen, right after he got released."

They sound like some vaudeville duo, Jon thinks. They must have rehearsed this explanation over and over, practiced it when they were alone and tried it out on the rare neighbors willing to listen. At his poolside, Bryce looks less like a favorite cousin and more like a guy trying to sell him a car.

"I didn't even have to do jail time, either. I could have gone to trial and got off with probation, but I pleaded guilty to keep her from having to testify and dragging it on. As long as she was eighteen by the time I got out, I was fine. Would've been harder to have to live with a restraining order. So I did four and a half years and who was there the day I get out?"

Kim bows as if accepting an award, then claps her hands together. Jon is glad to see they are, if anything, on the smaller side, no different than Jill's. The rest of her is broad-shouldered and athletic. She looks like she belongs in a gum commercial. "We really appreciate you understanding," she says.

"That's right. It's nice to finally have some friends. I swear, people love to judge. It takes just one person to check that list online and then the whole neighborhood turns. The looks I get, even when I'm just getting the mail… it hasn't been easy."

And here comes the soft sell, the sentimentality. What's worse, Jill is hooked deep. She's beaming there on the diving board, like she's hearing the world's greatest love story and not someone's excuse for doing time for child molestation. It's taken five minutes and Bryce is now his friend, the rest of his neighbors enemies. They've chosen sides and there's no going back. He knows this feeling, it's all too familiar, and for a second he wonders if it really is too late to apologize to Gayle and sign her damn petition.

"Isn't it exciting?" Jill whispers as he sits beside her on the board, both of them dangling their feet into the water.

"And don't you dare hire anyone to clean your pool," Bryce shouts. "Do not give that bitch the satisfaction. I'm sorry to be so heated but when someone threatens what I have, this life I've made, that's 100 percent legit now—I will defend myself however I have to. You just buy the chemicals and I'll come over once a week and do it. It's my pleasure." Bryce continues walking the pool's edge while Kim returns to her chair and lies on her back. The front of her thong is cut so narrowly that it's hard for Jon to focus anywhere else; she obviously shaves but hasn't for at least a couple of weeks.

"Maybe just have a cup of coffee waiting for me when I get done," Bryce says. "And hey, do you guys have any beer?"

THE BEERS LEAD TO drinks, and the drinks lead to dinner, more drinks, then dessert. "We may actually have friends," Jill says after the Bryces finally leave. It's already dark out and they're both naked in bed.

"I didn't think they were ever going to leave."

"They were fun," Jill says. "And she's so pretty, isn't she?"

"I guess, yeah."

"And he isn't creepy either, not like you'd think someone who did that would be."

"I really don't want these people in our lives," says Jon. "Honestly, I don't even know why we need anyone else, we never have before. And of all the people, a sex offender? I don't like the way this feels."

"You're acting like a baby. Let's not ruin this. We may actually have made friends."

"We don't want friends," he says.

"That's always been you. You don't want friends. You never want to make friends. I get bored when it's just the two of us."

Bored. She's bored, he thinks. She's bored and he had no clue. He assumed she was as satisfied as he was. At least the Bryces don't have kids, he thinks. Jill sees a kid and she starts in again with all that talk, all that drama.

"Let's just not get too chummy with them."

"We kind of have something in common," she says.

"We have nothing in common with them. I have nothing in common with him."

"I'm just saying. Given the circumstances, they aren't much different than us."

GOOD TO HIS WORD, Bryce arrives every Saturday. He shows up in the morning to clean the pool and Jill greets him with the beverage of his choice. She starts buying cantaloupes and muffins and when Kim comes over around noon they make a regular brunch of it, lounging around the pool, drinking beer and smoking pot, and when the sun gets too hot they go inside to watch TV or play board games or cards. Jill and Kim are always whispering about something and Jon pretends to care about the sports Bryce never shuts up about. They head back out to the pool in the afternoon, and sometimes they'll stay through the evening if there's a frozen pizza around, or when Bryce insists on ordering in. He can drink beer faster than Jon can drink water, while Kim prefers wine and has already drunk a bottle of white and is halfway through the red. Her hair is pulled back into a long, single intricate braid that Jill tied while they were all watching a Disney movie on television, the two women knowing the words to every song. Kim had sat Indian-style on the floor below the couch in her pink tank top and gray and pink camouflaged shorts, and with Jill playing with her hair she looked like she could've been their teenage daughter.

Jon uses the bathroom and looks at himself in the mirror. He looks higher than he feels, and the few days' stubble on his cheeks makes him look like he's already hungover. He's got to stop smoking, eventually. His thoughts aren't fuzzy but his knees are wobbly, they keep moving even as he stands still. But it's the thoughts, that's the worst part, how he can't shut them off. Jill hasn't said anything since that night but around this time every Saturday, when all he wants to do is lay down with her and nap or even just go to bed and not have to listen to anything or anyone, that word comes back to him: bored. Bored when it's just the two of us. It may have been her taking another angle on the baby issue, he thinks. She wouldn't be bored if there were three of them, and she wouldn't have to invite strangers over either. Still, there's the risk involved. He's told her about that.

When he comes out the bong is back on the coffee table and the room has a fresh, gauzy haze. Bryce is standing up and finishing a crude joke about a woman with a large vagina. "Forget about your flashlights, guys, just help me find my car keys and I'll drive all of us out of here!"

Jill laughs so hard she dribbles a mouthful of wine down her shirt. Kim takes another hit, then Jill again and back to Bryce and by the time it gets to Jon the ash has started to suck through. Just as well. It doesn't feel like two strangers in their house anymore, it's more like three, Jill sitting between the Bryces on the couch, laughing and drinking and him on the outside looking in, face pressed up against the glass.

"What's the date today?" Bryce asks. "Is it the sixteenth? It's the sixteenth, isn't it?" He raises his beer bottle and clinks the girls' wine glasses. "That means we've been here seven months now. Neighbors be damned, right? That bitch and her fucking petition. Hey, here's to having friends."

They all clink together and Jon looks for his beer but it's indistinguishable among all Bryce's empties on the coffee table. He clinks the shaft of the empty bong instead.

"I mean look at us. Do I look like a pedophile? You think people would hear a guy out, but not here, not in this country. And shit, they think statutory laws are going to keep girls from having sex?

They're just fucking other thirteen-year-olds and getting the wrong idea about it all, that it's supposed to be real fast and doesn't even feel good. What's the good of that?"

"We had sex when we were thirteen," says Jon, surprising himself. "Jill and I did. I think it was pretty good. Good enough that we're still having it, anyway."

"So you guys knew each other when you were thirteen?"

"We knew each other way before that. Our whole lives, really."

"We grew up near each other," Jill adds.

"The saddest thing is that we can't have kids," says Kim. "Fred can't be around kids, not as long as he's still on that list. He couldn't drop them off at school or even go to a park with them."

"Isn't that some shit?" says Bryce. "It's a joke, is what it is. It's bad enough they kept us apart for five years, now we can't even have our own kids? We got a lawyer working on it."

"We want children," Kim says. "I want children. How about you, Jon?"

It's all too much—the weed, the booze, this conversation and the way it's headed. Jon gathers some empties and heads into the kitchen, knowing that this will bring on the baby debate once again, and hell if he's going to talk about that in front of these people. He's showed her the research, the odds of the kid having webbed hands and feet, an abnormally large head, cleft palate, hip dysplasia. The odds of something happening. He can hear the three of them whispering in the living room, though, and whispering still even after Kim appears in the doorway.

"I'm sorry," she says. "I didn't mean to bring up a sore subject."

"It's okay. It's not a big deal."

"That's not what I've heard from Jill. She's told me before that she wants kids, but you don't."

"It gets a little more complicated than that."

"I know," she says. "I know all about the complications."

It's the alcohol that's kept him anchored, he realizes, washing away all the usual pot-paranoia that suddenly comes flooding back now that she's said this, now that it's out in the open, exposed. He feels the sudden need to check that all the doors are locked, to rip the doorbell off the wall.

"If a woman wants a child, Jon, there's not much you can do."

This is something he knows. It's something he can tell already, from the way she walks over to him, and the fact that the whispering has stopped in the living room. She takes his hand and puts it on her hip and she hugs him, she rests her head on his chest and they stand there in the kitchen holding each other. If there was only music, they could be dancing.

"You can't give her a baby," she says, "but you can give her this."

He could tell her so much. That he knows what separation feels like, what it's like to be forbidden the only person in the world you've ever loved, but the thought exhausts him. There's no need for talking right now. There will be more than enough time for that tomorrow. And then there's Monday after that.

MIHARA

三原山

Patrick Parr

FRIDAY NIGHT IS SUICIDE night and we've been coming the last five weeks. My buddy and I took the mountain rail and now wait on two people to fall into the pit. We've brought lawn chairs. We've paid 4000 Yen for six visits. So far twelve people have plunged into the hole, wide as two football fields, so deep you can't see the bottom. It is, officially, an abyss with a slight orangish glow you can only see with the strongest binoculars. That, the *shihainin* tells us, is the magma. Since 1933, the magma of Mt. Mihara has consumed over six thousand bodies. We are here to watch two more.

We're not alone. Every Friday around two dozen others bring their chairs and blankets. We all wait on a smooth flat rock about twenty meters wide. You would think it's a picnic. On the other side of the pit is a red tent where the Savior waits behind her table. Eric calls her that—The Savior. She will be the last person they talk to, these suicides. She will try and tell them that their lives are worth something, that things aren't as bad as they seem, that they need to hold on and survive.

The Savior is an old lady a shade under five feet with a hunched back and sparkling silver hair. Each week she's worn the same clothes: gray shirt and vest, black pants, and blue Converse All-Star shoes. Her success rate, by Eric's count, is 8 in 20. "Eight lives," he says. "All owed to her. Some of them will probably have kids, too."

We heard about suicide night from a man advertising the event at the bottom of the mountain. He handed me a flyer and walked two fingers off the edge of his palm, hoping us *gaijin* would understand. We didn't, but were curious enough to show the flyer to a co-worker fluent in Japanese. He offered a warning. "I haven't done it," he said, "but the people who go… they get addicted. If you're not careful, you will too."

Eric and I are both stuck in similar positions of depression. Our combined debt is over 81,000 dollars, our old girlfriends back home have moved on. The only real skill we have is our ability to speak English to people starving to understand the language, so they can have the chance to leave this island and start their own canyon of debt elsewhere. Nearing thirty, we have come to a humbling realization: We are, in every sense of the word, ordinary.

So we left our air-conditioned apartment full of video games and knockoff DVDs and have become regulars up here. The first Friday brought one man, middle thirties, still dressed in a dark blue suit and loosened tie. He talked to the Savior for twenty minutes, then shook his hands violently and kicked his metal chair. He ran to the edge and we stood with the crowd and moved in close. He jumped in feet first, arms flailing. He fell for over seven seconds, until he vanished into the murk. His disappearance activated something inside me that still, to this day, I cannot fully explain. Every part of my body felt electrically charged. This was no stunt. We had witnessed a man's final moments. Never had I seen anyone's final moment, at least not in reality.

For days we didn't talk about it, but it was on our minds. We quit video games. Killing cyber-zombies, shooting at digitized cops, felt more meaningless than it ever had before. Watching DVDs changed too. My favorite movie, about the mafia, seemed ridiculous now. Food tasted differently. I thought about what I was eating, how I was eating, why I was eating.

"What do you think finally did it?" Eric asked, days after.

"Maybe it wasn't just one thing."

Eric nodded. "I guess it's never just one thing, is it?"

THE NEXT FRIDAY BROUGHT two young women who held hands and wore blue and white high school outfits. It happened quickly this time. The Savior grabbed their arms and begged them not to do it. She held on strong enough that the girls pulled her over the table as they left. She fell into one of the metal chairs and they looked back and bowed, then peeked into the pit and let their bodies fall. They held each other as they fell and a sharp staccato shriek came out of one of them. Their bodies struck against a jagged rock and their bond was broken. I remember looking around at everyone else, faces blank as mine must have been. I have never seen someone cry on Mihara. If you were here you'd understand—this isn't about crying. This is about something else.

THE THIRD FRIDAY BROUGHT a group of six people, three women and three men. Eric used a pair of binoculars he'd bought from a pawn shop a block away from our conversation school. He watched them talking in the tent and assumed that they were couples, maybe married to each other. Young, good-looking, all of them in their twenties. The men had on shorts and sandals, the women sweatpants and tank tops. The Savior spoke to them for an hour. Two of the women broke down and were held, and eventually everyone went back down the mountain. The crowd whispered many things and then we left too.

Disappointment is not the right word for what I felt then. It wasn't emptiness either. Desolation, maybe; as if the whole experience had opened inside me something so large I couldn't begin to feel it. They had found a reason to live, and now my mind kept searching for reasons to die. Psychologists have written about compensatory energy, how our moods operate like a battery, how the excitement of another can cause negativity in you without knowing. They blame compensatory energy for a lot of things. For divorce mostly, and suicide—when everyone around is telling you, so positively, to cheer up, be happy, to let love back in your heart! When all you want to do is find someone on your level, someone who can feel to their very core the poison coursing through your thoughts. Someone with their own poison.

THE NEXT FRIDAY THREE women had their last conversation with the Savior. Two of the women sat Indian-style while the other walked close to the edge. Groups typically go in together or not at all, and I was about to tell Eric that the Savior had done her job again when she slipped and bounced into the pit, her body spiraling into the darkness. The quick scream she gave, the way her body twisted in the air, caused me to vomit. Two others, too. They call this *jisatsu sats-jin*, or a suicidal murder, and it rarely happens.

We reached the apartment and our white, formless couch.

"What did you think?"

"What do you mean?"

"Did you feel something?"

"What?"

"When—"

"Yeah, but feel what?"

"Like she was supposed to go in, whether she wanted to or not."

We had water on the stove and it had just started boiling.

"It was an accident."

"I know."

We ate pasta from the 100-Yen store and washed the pot and bowls. We watched people talking on TV and later, I caught Eric staring at himself in the bathroom mirror.

"I'm addicted," he said.

"I know," I said. "I know."

We threw out our zombie game and most of our DVDs. We sold the Playstation to our neighbor for 10,000 Yen. "That's fourteen more visits," Eric said. I stopped drinking alcohol. It made me feel good, and I didn't want to feel good, I wanted only to breathe, to appreciate the simple act of living and all the little efforts inside it. I started giving my English lessons with passion, and the students thanked me. "Your eyes change," they said. "Bigger." I was not about to tell them what caused it.

LAST WEEK A MIDDLE-AGED man in his forties came to the Savior wearing day-glo orange running shorts and a blue tank-top. It was raining, but the man didn't care and neither did we. He had climbed (as all possible suicides are made to climb, the rail only for spectators) barefoot up the mountain and talked to the Savior for just five minutes. He turned around and cursed us all for being here. At least I think he did. I heard the words *haji o shire,* or 'shame on you', and he pointed at us with fury, spitting in our direction and throwing rocks. He crossed his arms over his chest and hopped into the pit. It was almost comical, seeing him disappear after spewing so much venom.

WHICH BRINGS US TO today. I have been writing in this note-book as we wait for two businessmen to discuss their problems with the Savior. I've been obsessed with wondering what she says to them. Does she offer them religion? Some ancient wisdom? Or does she only listen? I can imagine her delivering one sentence: "Tell me your story... from the beginning." And they will tell her how they have come to such a decision, tell her of the inescapable darkness, how each second of their lives is now spent thinking about death. They are finished, they'll say. And she will nod and tell them that, yes, she feels that way too, that no matter how hard she tries or how many people she speaks to, she feels herself dying every day. Yet it's always my voice inside of her, saying how badly she wants to help people but can't help herself, and what, then, is the point in giving advice when she needs it too?

The two businessmen are sitting in metal chairs, each using their hands to emphasize something, as if they are pleading to keep their job but you know it's the exact opposite. They are spilling out whatever they can to show her that they are reasonably and emotionally dead. One man keeps talking, while the other walks with his head bowed to the edge of the cliff. He loosens his tie and takes off his sport coat and his white-collared shirt. From the coat he takes a small knife, what looks like a kitchen knife, and I swear for a moment he looks directly at me, at Eric and the rest of the crowd as he brings it above his head and with two hands plunges the blade into the center of his stomach. We hear him groan as his body, half-dead, gently falls into the pit, where he caroms off the side and drops swiftly into the black.

The other man looks over the edge and walks back down the mountain.

The Savior did the best she could.

I am doing the best I can.

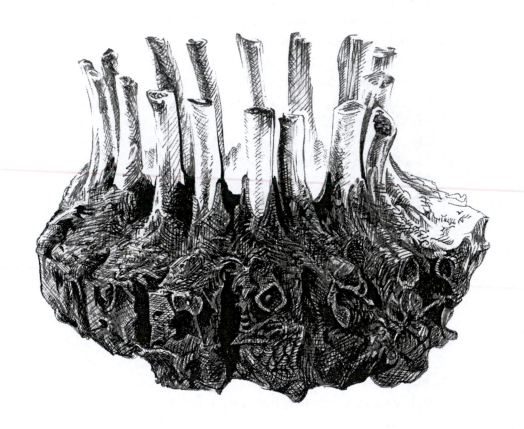

LODGERS

Ethel Rohan

FROM THE HILL, RORY could see over the fields to the farmhouse and parked there in the yard an unfamiliar car, a hunter green Morris Minor with a large black suitcase tied to its top. Mrs. Gillespie sometimes referred lodgers to the Deavitts whenever her guesthouse got full, and Rory mostly welcomed the occasional outsiders and the break they brought from the everyday, everyone aside from the mouthy Americans and the deadened married couples like his parents. But maybe here was someone closer to his age, he thought, from somewhere far beyond the monotony of Ballinshere. He cleared the distance between the fields and farmhouse in minutes, not even stopping to wash at the water pump.

Rory hesitated at the back door, hearing a rare excitement in his father's talk and the voice of this new visitor, soft in tone and the accent posh, from some choice part of Dublin. She thanked Rory's parents for agreeing to accommodate her, and Rory's father passed off the gratitude with an exaggerated laugh. Perhaps he'd opened a bottle of Powers for the guest, someone special so.

Rory scraped the muck from his Wellingtons on the steel doormat and entered the kitchen, stopping still when he saw her. There, at their scarred kitchen table, sat the most striking woman he'd ever encountered in the flesh. She looked to be older, mid-thirties maybe, with long black hair and a creamy, soft-boned face. The woman stopped mid-sentence and smiled at him, to which Rory could only blush and sputter a half-intelligible greeting. His mother sat opposite the woman, her expression hardening as Rory's cheeks filled with heat.

"Don't just stand there, Rory, fetch Mrs. Moore's things from her car."

"Please," she said, "call me Ashling."

Her smile found him again.

RORY HAULED THE THIRD and largest suitcase upstairs, conscious of Ashling climbing the steps behind him, the case heavy enough to hold all of his possessions put together. He tested her name silently, Ashling—the soft start of it and the little flick of the tongue at the end. The name meant 'dream' if he remembered his Gaeilge well enough. Not that he'd had much learning, his parents having pulled him from school two years ago so he could work the farm full-time. It was something he'd never minded much until now, when he wanted to draw out the words necessary to impress her.

Rory moved from the stairs and onto the landing, almost falling under the case's weight. He thought he heard Ashling snicker as they entered the guest bedroom and his cheeks blazed again.

"I'm sorry the cases are so heavy," she said, moving to the room's only window and letting in the malicious breeze and the stink of the silage. "It's really so beautiful here."

"You think?" said Rory.

She glanced at him quizzically then returned to the view. Alone with her in the small room, Rory felt especially self-conscious—his pimples bigger and whiter, his cow's lick ridiculous and stockinged feet too small. His big toe peeked through his threadbare sock, the nail yellowed. Worse, he smelled of hay, sweat, cigarettes and cow shite. No matter how hard he scrubbed, there would always be that stink of the farm on him. If she asked, he'd say he was eighteen.

"Thank you for your help," she said, her attention already on unpacking. From her largest suitcase she removed a checkered wooden case finished with a shiny lacquer and held together with bright brass hinges. "Do you play chess?" she asked.

Rory swallowed a childish impulse to mention his skill at checkers. He shook his head.

"I can teach you if you like?"

"You must be planning on staying a while so."

"I'm not in any hurry anywhere, no."

She unlatched the case and removed an assortment of gleaming chess pieces sculpted from blond and black woods. Her work, she explained, hand-carved from ancient bog oak. She gave him a few to examine—a castle and horse, and the crowned king with a finial at the tip that reminded Rory of a beggar's cupped hand. The horse, he noticed, even had teeth—tiny notches dividing each one. He fought the urge to pocket it.

"That's the knight, an important piece," she said. "You really should learn; it's a fascinating game."

He held the knight a moment longer in his large, dirty hand before dropping it to the bedspread.

"You don't seem enticed," she said. "What interests you then?"

"I dunno, really. I'm not one for making things, that's for sure."

She picked up a blond pawn. "Well, I don't think of myself as *making* them. It's as if they're already there in the wood—when I carve, all I do is set them free."

A waft of cow shite blew through the open window as she spoke. With eyes glazed she stared at the piece in her hands, a world away, thought Rory, even as she was right there in the room with him. Is this how he appeared to people—not at all? Rory felt the blood leave his face and like a fool checked the carpet at his feet, half-expecting to see a stain.

"Are you all right?" she asked, suddenly herself again.

"Why wouldn't I be?"

He looked down again at the carpet, sorry for his sharp words. Ashling resumed unpacking and in the stretch of silence that followed Rory's nerves got the better of him. At the doorway he reminded her his mother would have dinner ready shortly.

"She's not one to be kept waiting," he said.

In the shower Rory raked his fingernails over his body with especial vigor, digging into his armpits, groin, and the crack of his arse. He dressed in his best and hurried downstairs to the kitchen, where his mother looked him over with narrowed eyes and her lips pushed into a sour nub, an expression that scarcely cracked even as Ashling entered the room.

"We're having lamb," she said.

Rory's father said the blessing, after which a heavy silence descended. The smell of meat, mint and rosemary had built up in the kitchen, as oppressive as the leftover heat from the oven.

Rory's mother carved. "So you're from Dublin, Mrs. Moore?"

"A city girl, that's right. I hope you won't hold it against me."

"And you're travelling alone?"

Rory followed his mother's gaze to the pale skin circling the bottom of Ashling's ring finger.

"You've such a beautiful home," said Ashling.

"So you've said. And yours is where, did you say?"

Rory looked to his father, hoping he'd put a stop to this inquisition, but the man was oblivious, shoveling more meat and potato into his wet mouth.

"I'm afraid nowhere's home at the moment," Ashling said. "I'm keeping my options open."

"I see," said his mother, with an edge as serrated as her knife.

Ashling excused herself from the kitchen as soon as the meal finished. Rory's father remained at the table, worrying the carrot from between his teeth with his dirty fork. His mother curled a solider of bread and sopped up the last of the lamb's blood from her plate.

"She's a strange one, isn't she?"

Rory stood. "It's beyond me why anyone would pay to stay here and put up with you and your prying."

"Don't talk to your mother like that," his father said. "We charge a fair rate besides. Nothing she can't afford coming from Dublin." His parents carried on with their gossip while Rory washed the dishes with ferocity, smacking at the water in the sink and picturing there his mother's face. He barely noticed their conversation fall silent as Ashling returned to the room with the chess case in hand.

"Rory? How about that lesson?"

"Chess, is it?" said his father. "I used to play years ago. And look at this set!" He reached for the lacquered case and gushed at the carved pieces inside. "Lookit, Dolores! Aren't they something?"

"Tedious game," his mother said.

"Let's play, shall we?" He sprung from the kitchen with the chess case under his arm.

"It seems we shall," said Ashling, flashing to Rory another apologetic little smile as she followed his father into the living room.

HIS FATHER HAD REMAINED at the chess board until late that night, each of the old man's moves having taken far too long—his attention given more to the TV than the game. The next morning Rory lingered in bed before daybreak, fantasizing about Ashling in the room next to his. He burrowed deeper into the warmth of his sheets and repeated Ashling's name in a whisper, yet as much as he strained to hear some life from her room through the thin wall, there was only silence. He pictured her splayed naked on the guest bed, her lips parted and eyes thick with lust, her pale finger beckoning him. His hand moved into his shorts and he stroked himself to the rhythm of her name, *Ash-ling, Ash-ling*.

After milking the cows and returning the herd to the pasture, Rory and his father worked the hay fields all through the morning and into the relentless noonday sun. By early afternoon the much-awaited silhouette shimmered in the distance—Rory's mother come with the lunch, a large picnic basket pulling on the crook of her arm. As she neared, Rory shaded his eyes with his hand, confused at first by the slim, sculpted outline and then filling with excitement as he realized. His father greeted Ashling heartily and freed her of the weight of the picnic basket.

"I hope you're not vexed with me after last night?" he teased.

"Never," she said. "All's fair in chess."

Rory grabbed a ham and cheese sandwich from the basket and ate furiously. Why couldn't the old fool just go off someplace? Did he not realize how daft he sounded, not knowing that she'd let him win? She pitied him, Rory was sure. How could she not?

Ashling settled on the baked ground and leaned against the haystack between father and son, her shoulder brushing Rory's and sending electric charges down his arm.

"Are you up for another game this evening?" asked Rory's father. "I promise to go easy on you this time."

"I believe Rory wants his turn at besting me tonight."

"I doubt he even knows how to play, do you, boy?"

"You've no idea what I know."

Ashling sighed. "I envy you both, you know. It's just so beautiful here."

Again with her praise of this endless bog, thought Rory. Was there really anything to admire about these shite-filled pastures and dumb, plodding cattle? His father and mother too were blind to the truth of this place—a wasteland filled with shadows, dotted with rust-red barns and bone-white cottages all as dull as the people inside them.

Ashling reached into the picnic basket again and removed a short knife and a small piece of bog oak. She resumed carving what looked to his father like a doll with long wavy hair and a surprising life in its face.

"Not a doll," she laughed, "a mermaid." She went on to explain her process, how the rough cuts gave way to finer details, the several rounds of sanding required, and the coats of linseed oil necessary for the finish.

His father studied the mermaid-in-making. "Wasn't it Van Dyke who wrote *The Little Mermaid*?"

Rory cringed. "It was Hans Christian Andersen, you ape."

"What differ," said his father.

After a time, Ashling returned her mermaid to the basket, then stood and dusted off the buttocks of her faded jeans. "I think I'll take a walk down as far as the river." She pointed to a band of trees. "Just straight down there, right?"

Rory jumped to his feet. "I'll show you."

"You're not going anywhere." His father had his pitchfork in hand again and caught him by the shoulder. "We've a day's work to do yet. She can manage fine on her own."

The men returned home that evening to find a second car in the yard, a Hillman Avenger in dirty maroon. The contents of Rory's stomach turned to lead. If this was another guest, he'd have to give up his bedroom and sleep on the living room couch.

Peter Reid stood tall and broad-shouldered and hailed from Belfast. He showed to dinner dressed in brown loafers and a salmon-colored shirt buttoned low on his chest. The crop of dark hairs there seemed like wild, wiry creatures crawling up toward his neck and down his arms. Hard as Rory tried, it proved impossible not to like him. The man had a keen grin and playful manner, even if he did seem all too confident, as if his every word would meet with only favor. He also was the first person who cared enough to engage Rory in conversation like an equal, talking about the national and local football and all the fuss and spectacle around the moving statues down in Ballinspittle.

"Such shite," Rory said, supposing it what Peter would want to hear.

"You mind your mouth," said his mother. "It's not for the likes of us to say where and when heaven shows itself."

"Well it's certainly not around here."

"For that you deserve a zap of lightning!"

"Ah, leave him," said Peter. "He's a grand lad, a credit to you both."

Such a peacemaker, this Peter with his praise. Rory still couldn't help but wonder if it was anything but a posture put on by those from the city, like Ashling's fawning over the dry fields and the spindly trees. It hardly mattered anyway, as it wasn't long before Peter's attention had focused entirely upon Ashling and her occupation.

"A sculptor!" he cried. "I did woodwork in school. Wish I'd stayed at it."

"It's never too late," she said. "Our art never leaves us."

"Maybe you could give me a refresher course?"

"In woodwork?"

"For a start, yes."

"I suppose we could hunt down some bog wood around here," said Ashling. "That is if you don't mind, Mr. Deavitt."

"Of course he wouldn't," Peter said, wiping his mouth and leaving his napkin on the table. "We'd be doing him a favor clearing limbs. Shall we go, then?"

"Right now?" Ashling blushed as if asked to do something indecent.

"We are but lodgers," said Peter, as if on stage. "Now is all we have."

Rory's mother grew red as a radish. "You can't go anywhere yet," she spluttered, "the dinner's not finished and I've yet to serve dessert! Worked on those apple tarts all afternoon, I did."

"I'm sorry, Mrs. Deavitt," said Peter, "but I'm afraid I'm giddy this evening and can't be contained by a chair or house or even such a fine meal and company as this. Are you ready, Ashling?"

She slipped from the table and Rory watched them leave, the two of them arm-in-arm and tittering together like a couple from some previous century about to dance in the royal court.

"Can't imagine they'll find anything but blindness at this hour," said his father.

"May they catch a chill, the stupid fools."

Rory said nothing, but thought about the mess of food in his stomach, the beef and the veg like the farm itself inside him, and the acids going at everything, making it all disappear.

B Y THE TIME ASHLING and Peter returned, Rory's parents had long retired and he'd set up bed as best he could on the couch. If they noticed him there they didn't let on, but continued straight upstairs, tripping and laughing and reeking of drink. They'd closed Flatherty's together for sure. Rory punched the cushions on the couch, both in efforts to get comfortable on the lumpy relic yet also needing to hurt something.

Sometime deep that night, during one of the many spells when Rory started awake, the floorboards upstairs creaked and a bedroom door eased open. He had expected as much—the whispers that followed, and the low rustling after the door was closed. He stayed as long as he could bear on the couch before struggling from his tangle of blankets and sneaking up the stairs. Outside the guest bedroom he paused and held his head as close to the door as he dared. The bed frame squeaked faster and louder. Then came muffled panting, gasping, and a small moan followed by cold silence.

Rory remained in the hall, breathing hard, when the bedroom door pulled open. The boy stared past Peter in the doorway to Ashling naked on the bed, her black hair fanning the pillows just as in his fantasies. Her breasts were so much smaller than he'd pictured, but her nipples almost glared with an unimagined darkness and the tuft of black hair between her legs recalled Peter's chest, thick and wild, like something alive. It was the first time Rory had seen a naked female in reality. Her eyes locked with his and he thought she smiled before covering up.

Peter pulled the door closed behind him and stood much too close.

"Go back to bed, son."

On the couch Rory chafed himself raw as many times as he could through what remained of the night, moving in and out of a troubled sleep and awaking early in the morning to his mother's shouts from the kitchen. His father, with a tired voice of defeat, tried to calm her as she ranted about sin and damnation and curses on the house. "She said she might stay two weeks or more," he pleaded. "We need the money."

"I'm sure it's her money you're worried about."

After several more rounds, they appeared to reach a compromise and Rory's father mounted the stairs. A short time later, Peter clattered down with his few belongings and banged the front door closed.

Rory, still in his pajamas, plodded into the kitchen. His mother's eyes were red-ringed and her cheeks wet and shiny. "That Peter," she spat, "you're not to turn into a dirty article like him, do you hear me!"

At mid-morning Ashling appeared late to breakfast. Rory and his parents had already begun the morose meal when she knocked on the kitchen door and slipped into her chair at the table, her mouth skewed into a sort of silent apology.

Rory's mother did not hesitate. "I'm sure you'll have noticed, *Mrs.* Moore, that we sent Peter packing. This is a God-fearing house and there'll be no more of the disgusting goings-on we had to endure here last night. Is that clear?"

Ashling looked down at her plate, her hands locked, prayer-like.

"I might also add," his mother said, "that I find the sculptures in your room offensive and I'll thank you to take them down and put them away."

"Now then," said his father, "her work is her own business."

"It's disgusting."

"It's bog wood in ways no one's thought of it before," he said. "How's that mermaid coming along, anyway?"

"Well, thank you. I'm almost finished."

His mother's jaw unlocked. "That has tits too, does it?"

Ashling drew a long breath and looked both furious and on the verge of tears. Rory lifted his foot under the table and kicked his mother hard on the shin. She roared and bucked in her chair as Rory bolted out the back door, his father's shouts chasing him, demanding he return.

WHEN HE ARRIVED AT the river his chest felt about to burst. He dropped to the riverbank and while his breath calmed he skimmed pebbles as best he could through hot tears. If his parents had their way he'd be stuck on this farm forever, just like the stony soil beneath him. Any mention of ambition aside from the farm infuriated his father and elicited scorn from his mother.

"What else would you do?" his father would say.

From his mother, "Where else would have you?"

Someone moved behind him and he spun around. Ashling—she'd followed him, just as he hoped and expected her to. She sat down on the grass beside him and smoothed her skirt on her thighs. She smelled sweet and foreign, of coconut, he realized.

"I'm leaving," she said. "I think it's best."

Rory fired another pebble, refusing to look at her.

"You're not much of a talker, are you?"

He reached for a stone, something larger.

"The dark, brooding type." She nudged a shoulder against his, and even this small touch gave him the same pain-pleasure charge he knew from the electric fences. The throb settled in his chest. Ashling got to her feet and moved to the river's edge, where she squatted and moved her finger through the water, tracing some design. He recalled the mermaid she was carving, how the hair fanned across its narrow back and was crowned in a headband of tiny sculpted flowers. She had said she set the sculptures free, that they already existed in the wood.

"What happened to your husband?" he asked.

"I left him."

"Why?"

Her finger resumed its travels through the water. "Because there was no good reason left to stay."

The tightness in his chest worsened, like giant hands flattening his lungs. His head, too, felt like it would cave in. She pulled her finger from the river and smiled back at him. "I drew something, see?"

He looked at the water and shrugged.

"Come on," she said. "You're not even trying."

"Don't be stupid," he said. "There's nothing there."

Wasn't she smart with her illusions—making things out of nothing and nothing out of things, her sculptures from dead limbs and oh, the beauty of bare soil and the bouquet of cow shite. He lifted a rock up over his head and threw it into the river. Ashling drew back from the splash.

"You don't just leave someone," he said. "You don't just walk away, like it all meant nothing. We can't just up and leave when-ever—"

"This was a mistake. I should go."

"Good!" he said, "Go! I never want to see you again."

She passed up the slope of the riverbank and he spun around reaching for her but she pulled her arm free. Rory grabbed her waist then and though she slapped at his arms he tightened his hold and wrestled her to the ground. He stretched himself on top of her and pinned her arms and legs. She tossed her head from side to side, grunting and shouting. He forced her lips apart with his own and pushed his tongue hard against the slick ridges of her gritted teeth, knowing that if he only tried hard enough, he could work his way into her.

TIMBER

Dan Micklethwaite

MARCUS WHALEY TOOK TO photographing the fallen trees. Close-ups and from a distance. Prints piled on his mantelpiece, on the desk beside his single bed.

He did this at first in the mornings before he clocked on. Standing on the drying pinecones, the needles, and the leaves of other, smaller trees. Looking down at the debris left from yesterday's work, the trunks not yet cut, but piled into pyramids and left on open dirt to cure and dry.

He started with one of those old square format cameras, held down near his waist with the viewfinder open on top like a laundry chute. He'd take his one or two pictures, wrap the camera loosely in a rag and put it away in his big steel lunchbox. It would stay there, beside his red and green chequered thermos, until he clocked off and until the other loggers went either homewards or to the bar just down the way. Marcus was an *I'll meet you later* kind of guy; he'd stay and take another couple shots. Catch the sap congealing on the stumps of trees that had been the last to tumble. Maybe snap one, two of a ruined birds nest tilted on its side and on the ground. Snap the shutter with a mournful press, somehow tender under all the calluses.

The shots would keep him awake for nearly an hour after his head hit the pillow. Awake and contemplating how his pictures would turn out, how the felled trees would translate into black and white. He may have spent a given day up in the arms of high branches, or straddling the root-strewn feet as he sawed; may have been aching and carrying a weary tingling in his muscles and his head from never quite taking on enough water. But he would always, those first few months, lie there and consider and imagine and put off his sleep.

At the end of each week, and before Friday night's drinking, he would head to the drugstore in town where the man would develop the film he delivered in little black tubes. And each Saturday morning he'd walk over again to see that man, squinting because those Saturdays were always too bright, and collect his envelope full of prints.

He'd spend the rest of the weekend looking over the results, marveling quietly at the way one or two of the photos looked as if they'd be at home in a newsstand magazine. Then he'd go to Mae's Diner to eat, come home at seven and sleep like the dead.

Three, four, five months this went on, this pattern of living. By that fifth month his photographs were getting more adept technically, were looking more and more like magazine-cover fare. But the extra hour that he had to wake up every weekday morning, the extra hour he stayed on site at each day's end, it started to eat at him, like termites in his frame.

It happened without his noticing at first, the way such infestations always took a hold, but then he did notice and the thoughts he didn't want came in. Thoughts of how this was just a hobby and that word—hobby—like a child's game, like stamp collecting or doing tricks on a bike, that word took chunks from his legs and he felt nervous and unsteady every time he unwrapped his camera from the rag. He didn't want it to be a hobby, didn't want to think that he was thinking about it all that much. He didn't want that one thing he enjoyed to be seen the same way as part-time things that other people did.

You were a team on site, he knew. You were a team and that meant you were one and the same. Not outside, though. Not off-site. You were a man on your own and you needed to have a passion that made your mind a different thing to any other.

So he hung on, after those first months. He carried on spending just a little bit too much of his wages on film, and carried on getting up an hour early for as long as he could.

Six and three-quarter months and he stopped that, though. Six and three-quarter months and the back problems began and that extra hour before rising helped fight off the worst of the pain. But he still brought his camera to the site each day, inside his big steel lunch-box, and tried to take photos on whatever breaks he could find.

The quality dipped; the photos were not the same. The noise, the industry of the site when it was crowded, it grated on his nerves and screwed his focus. Each new picture looked like the picture before. Nights he still lay awake, only he now lay awake with worry. Thoughts like I'm burnt out, I've wasted whatever it was I had, they found him and he was easy prey.

His back got worse. He took sick days, after a nineteen-month stretch of going without. The foreman began calling him over for little chats. Gave him his first formal warning and sent him home for the rest of the week—this was a Wednesday—for misjudging the direction of a fall and wrecking a pile of logs stacked and ready for collection.

Marcus Whaley went days without photographing anything at all. He felt slipping the desire to take any more. Yet, back at work, he found himself watching the actual process of collapse, really watching it, more closely than he ever had before. The warning he'd been given made him all the more diligent, more anxious to avoid any further errors. And through this renewed attention to his job, he found a fresh focus.

He wasn't foolish in any way, and never would have tried this with a tree he'd been cutting, but he took to photographing trees as they fell. On breaks he'd wander through the site and find a spot where someone was still working. He would drink from his red and green checked thermos and hold his camera ready, waiting for the shout and the opening strains and then the bonecrack that signalled a trunk coming loose.

For a few weeks, the pain in his back improved. No more sick leave or accidents and he looked forward again to the walks into town to collect his prints on too-bright Saturday mornings. And on those prints were dark grey streaks, arcing through the backdrop of a balding forest like rainbows with all the colours taken out. They seemed illicit somehow, and enlivening thereby, those prints of dying pines.

Then the foreman caught him. Called it reckless endangerment. Put him on probation, but Marcus couldn't stop. Ten months in and he was fired, and there wasn't another logging firm for miles who'd agree to take him on.

In the weeks after that he would stand on the hillside across town and record with each new day the ways in which the woodscape changed. More blank spaces, like broad bare dunes pockmarked with dark green scrub. Some days tall, lone trees left in those spaces, the ones they hadn't had chance to give the cut before dusk and clocking off time came. Like a ship's masts, some of them, beached antiques, living wood left soon to tumble.

He didn't take his steel lunchbox with him anymore, but carried the camera from his front door to his standing place, a grassy slope set beside a doglegged streak of undergrowth and well clear from the interrupting shade of other trees. The camera bounced in a jagged way as he walked, thumping against his gut a second out of time with the rhythm of his steps. The more often he walked this route, the redder the flesh around his navel.

At nights he'd sit, hunched forward to ease the pain in his back, and bearing through the soreness beginning upon his stomach, leafing through selections of his photographs. He'd start at the first attempts he'd made and move through to the most recent, charting his improvement, the evolution of his eye. Congratulating himself with sips of sourmash, until he could no longer afford to pick up bottles from the store.

He stacked the empties around the lamp that occupied the back-left corner of his desk. In the evenings before sleep he'd experiment with alternative arrangements, play around with shutter speeds to try and coax the light onto the film in different, elasticated ways. Some nights this carried on beyond midnight, and he didn't make it out onto the hill until the following afternoon. He chastised himself for this, for missing the morning's finer light, so much better was it than the half-dark pall left by the sun as it slumped west behind the timber hill. He bullied himself, resolved to cut this late-night habit short. Rarely did he meet this resolution.

He started a kind of ration list, planning out what he could afford to spend on food in order to have cash left for further visits to the developers. The less he ate, the more his back pain worsened. The soreness about his navel had become a true bruise, dark blue and the skin pale around it. More frequently he would drift off, lose focus in the middle of a shoot, slip unready into sleep in the long grass of the hill. Waking then later on to find the trucks already hauling off the few barky carcasses weathered and dry enough to be put to further use. Frustrated, he would watch the skyline at those times, and consider the framing angles of his vision, without the lens, and daydream in a fractured fashion about getting famous for all this somewhere down the line.

He required a source of income, he decided, upon the realization that he was not just drifting off but passing out. He spent his evenings then being tougher with the judgements he doled out to each new batch of prints, and the negatives themselves, which he held against the lampshade and squinted at to check that no mistakes had been made in developing. That no pressing details were missing, nothing valuable somehow mislaid.

He made a gathering of twenty and took them to the Post Office, bought an envelope, and asked kindly for an address at which he might reach National Geographic or some comparable publication.

Marcus Whaley took to waiting whilst the clerk searched the brightly-lit square of his screen.

NEW BABY

Joshua Kleinberg

"TED KENNEDY IS PROBABLY GOING TO DIE SOON."

I don't know why I say this, except that it's true, or at least I believe it to be true. It is 2008 and he has a malignant brain tumor.

Sol told me this morning he thinks it's karma for the shit he pulled at Chippaquiddick. I was surprised Sol even knew about Chippaquiddick, surprised he could use "karma" in a sentence. I don't believe in karma, but I sort of like Ted Kennedy and wish he wouldn't die. It's so hard to tell with politicians.

"Ted Kennedy's a goner."

Sol and his wife Rebecca are at work, and I am slouched into their white sofa in their white living room, where no one can hear me say that Ted Kennedy is probably going to die soon. The TV is on, and I suspect if there were secret CCTV cameras in the house, the way I sometimes imagine, that my eventual viewers—from the CIA or Al-Qaeda or whoever—might think I'm watching a news report about Ted Kennedy, but I am not. I am watching The X-Files, which always seems to be on.

Gillian Anderson slams her car door. She is pissed. David Duchovny follows her out, explaining something. I want them to make love, but their haircuts are too old. I don't think they make love until the sixth season. Or I don't know, maybe they never make love.

I swing open the fridge door and stare inside for a while. I think: *orange juice*. Rebecca would have a fit if she saw me drinking from the carton, but she's a diabetic and won't drink it anyway, and Sol never minded until he got a wife. After the juice I stare some more and pick out a new jar of pickles. It opens with a satisfying *thwock*. The pickles are sliced longways and I deliberate far too long before plunging my pincered fingers in. The pickle slips out all bent and decrepit, like a little graffiti "J" with a stubby, spinal tail of a stem. It must've snuck past the quality-control ladies, all of them lined up in their hairnets—old women no doubt, cracking shriveled pickle jokes about their first husbands.

"David Duchovny is a really attractive guy."

I say this as I sit back down with my J pickle, and I wonder if I say it because I'm gay, but I think it's just because I'm jealous. I eat my pickle and am briefly glad it's a sliced and not whole pickle, because whoever ends up watching those tapes might jump to conclusions if I called David Duchovny attractive and then went and deep-throated a big long dong of a pickle.

"I'm not gay," I tell them, just in case.

I go upstairs to the guest room where I've been sleeping. I check my email, check my Facebook, re-check the email and then check my Facebook again. I post on my mother's wall a funny report from her local paper's police blotter: someone stole an old lady's toaster oven as it was cooking a frozen pizza. I imagine the incredulous police dispatcher. I imagine the 911 call and chuckle a little, annoyed with the elderly woman in her sad little single-room apartment.

I should say this now: the reason I am at Sol's is because my girlfriend and I broke up. And because I had moved into her apartment just a month before and given all of my furniture, most of my clothes, and many of my electrical appliances to the Salvation

Army, there was little else to do but make that sheepish phone call and ask him for a place to crash. The last time Sol and I had spoken was over a casket at our Uncle Lyndon's wake. We stood over the smirking dead man without looking at each other.

"He was a good guy," said Sol.

"He used to hit us with his King James Bible," I said.

"That was once. And he never hit you."

"He was too old by the time I was smart. He did throw a glass of milk in my face the once."

"He was good," Sol said. "I didn't say he was great."

I GUESS YOU DON'T REALIZE how dysfunctional you can become until you actually get to work on it. I haven't changed my shirt in three days, haven't showered all week. I check my email again and decide to change shirts, but not to shower. Showering requires all sorts of commitments I'm not willing to make right now.

"This isn't because of Maggie," I say aloud, in the mirror, and the lights overhead sputter a little. "At some point," I say, "you'll be as happy as you are sad right now. The law of probability ensures it, if not God or whatever."

But I don't really think that's how it works—like life is some kind of sine wave, with peaks and valleys of happy and sadness. I think if you were to visualize emotion it'd be more like a color palette, like MS Paint, maybe. And right now I'm some dark green-ish babyshit color, because there's no way to be entirely black—no one's ever been that unhappy. You'd off yourself once you got anywhere near navy blue. And no one's ever been completely white, either. Unless that's an orgasm, which I think might be true, until I remember how disappointing orgasms usually are.

"Sadness," I say, "is as impermanent as happiness," but I don't think I believe that either. There is sadness, I think, and then there is leaving sadness, tucking sadness into a closet like a winter coat while you make vague wedding plans, take trips to folksy wineries in the country. Maybe all there is just sadness or killing time.

"Who the fuck would steal some old lady's pizza?"

THE ALARM SYSTEM BEEPS and I hear keys clanging downstairs. Sol is home and calling up at me. He says Rebecca has a thing, his day was hell, something about my undone dishes, something else. I'm not listening. I've plugged "happiness scale" into Google and am browsing around Cafepress for products marked Lao Tzu.

Sol plods up the stairs, repeating everything he's just said word for word. "And dude," he says at the door, "those pickles were for a barbecue."

"There's a lasagna bandit on the loose in mom's neighborhood."

He sits down on the bed, picks up our family picture on the nightstand, and looks at it sadly. "I'm really gonna miss her," he says.

"What do you mean? She's not dying."

"She will someday. And then I'm gonna miss her."

"Did you know there are 5,190 results for Tao Te Ching products on Cafepress?"

"What's Tao Te Ching?" he says.

"It's a philosophy. Like the yin-yang and stuff."

"Oh," Sol says. "What's Cafepress?"

"People upload things onto T-shirts and you buy them. Can you imagine someone actually buying a shirt that says 'We shape clay into a pot, but it is the emptiness inside that holds whatever we want'?"

"Speaking of shirts, Rebecca says I need to get a new one for this barbecue on Sunday. Do you want to, like, come with...?"

He's considering adding "me" to the end, which is agonizing for the both of us. This is my brother.

"Sure," I say. "I'll get you some more pickles."

SOL LIVES IN THIS upper-middle class suburb of the city we grew up in. About a half a mile from his townhouse is a colossal shopping plaza, one of those commercial utopias with its own stop signs and four-lane access roads. Sol insists that we walk, because gas is back up and a little exercise will do me good. He says I've been depressed and I say, "No I haven't."

The area is built for cars—no sidewalks—and we have to walk on the broad slope of grass beside the road. It feels good, I think, feels like being a kid again. I wonder if Sol feels like that.

"This feels good," I say.

"What feels good?"

"The grass. The slope of it."

"Seriously, dude. I think you're depressed."

"I just said it feels *good*." I change the subject. "So where is Rebecca?"

"With her parents," he says. "She's over there all the time lately. Not that I mind, I guess."

Not that I mind, either. It's not that I don't like Rebecca, it's just that neither of us really seem that interested in getting to know the other. She's short with me and she's a little too quick to join in when Sol and I gripe about our folks, but I know I'm putting them out. Sol had to assure me when I first moved in that it wasn't my fault she was always at her folks' house, that she goes there all the time.

"She even sleeps there sometimes," he said.

It smells clean in the TJ Maxx, like packaging and cologne samples.

"I'll try to make it quick," Sol says.

"Take your time," I say, as pleasantly as possible. I pick up a Jim Beam barbecue set and turn it over in my hands.

"They have food here too," Sol says. "Like fancy jarred things in the back. You should look, maybe they have pickles." He heads into the menswear section while I play with plastic-swathed iPod accessories up front.

I examine a footbath, a wine cozy, a picture of a pear. I'm looking at a dark leather "gift box" with a pen and keychain when Sol taps my shoulder and asks me to choose between the shirt he is wearing and the one in his hand. They are both blue-checkered shirts with short sleeves. Their patterns are nearly identical. He asks if I'll come with him while he tries on the other and tell him what I think.

Both shirts fit him weirdly—the first in the arms, the second in the waist. The first shirt is from St. John's Bay. The other is from FUBU. I tell him to get the FUBU.

"It'll be a conversation piece," I say.

But his attention has turned to a rack of toddler shoes just outside the dressing rooms. "Look," Sol says, "they make Chuck Taylors for babies now. They got little black ones and pink ones."

"They've been making them for years. Remember when Gary's kid was small? For his first birthday, they got him a pair of Jordans."

"Yeah," Sol says, "I forgot about him. How old do you think he is now?"

"Thirteen, maybe?"

"What do you think he's like?"

"I don't know," I say. "Probably horny and sad."

Sol doesn't laugh. He's moved on to a pair of miniature Timberlands, little stylish hiking boots that could fit in your palm. He seems frustrated with them, working them in his hands, testing the inflexibility of the sole. "How do they expect a kid to walk in these fucking things?" he says.

"I don't think they're supposed to."

He looks at me with a tired sneer. "Whatever," he says, dropping them back.

W E CHECK OUT AND return to the parking lot. Sol waits with a hand in his pocket as I smoke my last cigarette.

"What now?" I ask.

"I could eat," he says. "You hungry?"

I'm not. I can still feel the orange juice sloshing around in my stomach. I picture the pickle floating around like a raft.

"Let's do Rita's," he says.

"Oh, god."

"What's wrong with Rita's?"

"Nothing," I say. "It's fine."

"You do this with every damn restaurant," he says.

"I do this with every restaurant with *you*, because you only eat at these shitty, market-tested chains."

"Fine then. Where does baby Tyler want to eat?"

"Jesus," I say, "I didn't realize you were so invested. Let's just go to Rita's." I try to give him a look of retreat, but he's not paying attention. He's looking vacantly at his shoes as we walk.

The restaurant is just across the parking lot. It's the color of manila paper and made of what I assume is a cheaper imitation of stucco. Three stripes of red, white and green neon run around the tops of the walls, twisting to spell *Olé!* and *Viva!* I try to think of a Mexican hero to tell how he must be turning in his grave, but the only Mexicans I can think of are Vicente Fox and Pablo Escobar.

The sign reaches a hundred feet in the air and features a giant stemmed glass. "Rita's Bar and Grill," Sol explains, when he sees me looking at it. "Short for *marga*ritas."

"I caught that," I say, embarrassed that I hadn't.

It's dark as night inside. The place is lit by these half-watt strings of lights dripping flaccidly over every table. The hostess asks if we'd prefer a table or a booth, but Sol says we're going to sit at the bar. I knew this.

I knew we'd sit at the bar because Sol is in love with the bartender, Jess, whose hair is that kind of blond that's really off-white, and whose eyebrows are arched like commas, and who wears baseball shirts with cleavage cut into them. I knew all of this because Sol comes here nearly every week, comes home drunk and tells me how much he loves Jess, how blond her hair is and how pretty her eyes. He loves her because he's drunk and he thinks he should love her, and because she is not Rebecca, who has a weird nose and flyaways atop her head, and who lately seems to hate everything. If they lived by a T.G.I. Fridays, he'd love some brunette with big eyes, too.

Jess spots us from the back of the bar. She yells, "My favorite alkie!" and prances over with a big fake smile and her arms held out. They share an awkward over-the-bar hug and it grosses me out the way he brightens so visibly, like he's just now filling with blood.

"Who's this?" she asks, channeling something pornographic with the look she gives me. I think, *Shit*. Her tips must be ridiculous.

"This is my little brother, Tyler," Sol says. "He'll have a Flaming Blue Lamborghini, and I'll take a—"

"No," I say. "I thought we were eating."

"We are, dude. Get whatever you want. I'm buying." He says this more to Jess than to me.

"I'll have a drink. Nothing on fire."

On the back wall is a series of slush machines, each with a swirling porthole of color and a white bar rotating like radar. "Then get the Blue Venus," Sol says, "or get whatever you want." He hands me a spiral-bound menu that declares "It's Time to Get Rita'ed!" It's full of cartoon-colored drinks sweating in glasses big as bowls.

"Anything, man. Like I said—"

"I know. You're buying."

Sol orders a Blue Venus. What I want is a bourbon, not because it's my drink, but because it seems somehow pure in a place like this. I point to something green in a martini glass on page 14. "What's in this?" I ask Jess, but Sol pulls the booklet away. "Says right here, man. Vodka, peach Schnapps..."

"Alright, I'll just—"

"coconut rum, sweet and sour..."

"What about—"

"...pucker."

"Mango-ritas are half off," Jess says, picking some lint off her chest.

"A mango-rita sounds great." I mean this as concession to Sol, but he's not listening. He is watching Jess's panty-line crease within her jeans as she bends for the rum.

"So," he says. "Maggie."

"Jesus, Sol. I haven't even gotten my drink yet."

"Jess," he tells her mid-pour, "make it strong for my brother, here. We're nursing a break-up."

She looks over at me and pouts.

"Tell her about it, Ty. Get her perspective."

And I do—sort of. "She stopped laughing at my jokes," I say. "She stopped laughing at my jokes the second we moved in together, and I knew it didn't have long."

Jess says, "That's hard," and I hate it. She is wiping a glass and I hate that she can invest nothing in this conversation yet say something so trite and still comfort me, just by virtue of being pretty and not running off.

I tell them about it all—about the trip to the winery, about the pictures she'd make me take, how she hated to hold hands and how, at the end, I used to try so hard to make her happy. And when I'm finished, I am surprised by how much I like the mango-ritas. Sol is already reeling after his first Blue Venus. He shouts at intervals what he thinks are appropriate, supportive things; he calls Maggie cold, calls her a bitch, and I know he means no offense, it's just that comforting is not a thing he knows how to do. It's been this way most of our adult lives. He is trying, trying so hard to connect with his brother, over something, anything.

Something, I think. Anything.

Sometheen. Ennytheen.

And I realize, I am Rita'ed.

SOL HAS MOVED ON to Miller Lites and I have moved on to the bathroom, not vomiting thank God, but considering the possibility. When I leave I can see from across the bar that Sol has taken up with some other barmates, some guys with baseball caps and baskets of buffalo wings, and I think of how I sincerely imagined having a meal with my brother. I head for the door.

Outside it's brighter than the bar, the streetlights dropping their orange glow all around. Out back of the restaurant, the leaking cylinders of used cooking oil have given the concrete a perpetual glimmer and the dumpsters have a condensed smell of Mexican food that is not entirely disagreeable. I find Jess, smoking, fenced in by chain-link. She's sitting on a bucket and smoking like a man—like a sailor or a tattoo artist or something—so fast and so hard. And her hair, it's this smooth plane. A smooth plane of something well-conditioned and cared for. She looks at me like it means something. I am starting to see why Sol loves her.

"The gate's locked," she says. "Or I'd let you in."

"Could I bum a smoke?"

She cocks an eye and glares. "You just broke the cardinal bar rule. You never ask your bartender for a smoke."

"Oh," I say. "I'm sorry."

She pulls out her pack. "You realize I spend more time here than at home, right? If I can't smoke in peace here, there can't *be* any peace."

She passes a cigarette and her lighter through the links. The lighter is green, a pale green like an Easter egg, and I don't think I've ever seen another lighter this color. I light up and ask how her night's going, like, really going.

"It's fine. Good tips. Your brother always tips good."

"Yeah," I say. "He's a pretty good guy."

"Do you believe that?"

"What do you mean?" I say.

"I mean, do you really think your brother's a good guy?"

"He's got a wife," I say. I don't know why.

"Of course he does. This is fucking Rita's. Everyone's got a wife. He doesn't take his wedding ring off when he comes here, if that's what you think."

"That's exactly it," I say. "He's not like those other jerks at the bar. He gets along with them, but he's not one of them, you know?"

She puts her cigarette out on the heel of her shoe. "I'm not saying he's one of those guys. But he's kind of an asshole, right? Like, why is he here every week? Why isn't he at home with his family?"

"*I'm* his family."

"That's the only reason I bring it up," she says. "I've seen you; you cringe at everything he says. It's like you can't stand him. But great, so he's with family tonight. What about his wife? What's she doing? What's she doing all the other nights he's here?"

She lights another cigarette and waits. "Well I'm sure he hasn't told you," I say, and I want this to hurt her, but I know that it won't. "Sol and his wife had a kid. Kind of. They had a baby, a fetus. It was dead, though. And it had been dead. It was inside her for two days."

They had named him and everything. Jonathan. They moved into that townhouse with the second bedroom, the new baby's bedroom, then a guest room, now my bedroom, because the new baby never came.

"They just never recovered from it. They tried for awhile after, but nothing really worked—the baby or marriage or anything. He's floating along, and she's floating along. It will be over soon, which is good. It should be. It needs to be."

"Jesus," Jess says, and we both put our cigarettes out on our heels, in accidental unison, and stand there for a second.

"I met Maggie in a place like this," I say.

She says, "I've got to go back in."

S OL IS BENT TO the side, leaning hard on the bar, talking to the baseball capped dudes. One of them is grunting over Sportscenter. "Where have you been?" Sol asks, and all the baseball caps are looking on. "This is my brother, Tyler," he tells them. "He's going through a rough time right now."

The guys all nod. There's a baseball game on another TV, and we watch it. By the end of the eighth inning, Sol puts his forehead flat on the bar. "Man, we are so fucked," he says, and I mistakenly think he's talking about the game.

"I'm going to divorce my wife," he says.

"I'M GOING TO DIVORCE MY WIFE, DO YOU HEAR?" He screams this at me and the bar and whoever else can hear and I hate him for it. A baseball cap says "Fuck yeah!" I could kill him and my brother both. Jess is cleaning a spill further down the bar; she ignores them, betrays nothing. And I can see now how she is the best at what she does, a grade A bartender. She wants Sol to die and Sol will never know.

I say to Sol, "You're drunk."

I say it quietly, like it's some fucking secret.

WE WALK THE HALF-MILE home without speaking, with only the awkward rhythm of Sol's plastic bag swishing, the crumpled bulk of the shirt hitting the fronts, then the backs, of his knees.

It isn't so late and a few cars still sweep past, but the stoplights have all switched over to blinking yellows, and the sprinklers have finished their nightly program, soaking the grass in hard water. I push my hands into my pockets and try to be the lesser drunk, keeping pace with the crunch of Sol's bag, fixing my gaze down onto the grass that squishes like swampland.

We reach the neighborhood and somewhere on the sidewalks there I begin to quit hating my brother. Somewhere, I begin to feel sad. I think about Maggie and I'm not even sure what her face looks like anymore. I want to tell Sol, but when I look over at him I see a little halo of sweat staining his underarm and I don't.

When we get in, it's not even ten o'clock. Rebecca is still with her parents, watching a movie, probably. Probably dozing off while the male lead kisses whomever in the rain. I am relieved for this. I am glad she's not home.

Sol closes his eyes at the sink and fills a dirty cup with tap water then dumps it out and hands it to me, asking if I will warm him some milk.

His eyes are so big, like Muppet eyes, or anime. He heads to the living room and I hear the lights click on—every light in the room, in four separate clicks—as I watch the milk spin around in the microwave.

He calls from the sofa. "I wasn't just being drunk," he says. "I really am going to ask her for a divorce."

"I know."

"I just don't love her."

"I know," I say, and I am still sad, because this is my brother, drunk on the couch, trying to confess these things to me. It feels good though, this sadness, like a fire purging rot from the forest.

The microwave punches through with an acrid little beep and I bring the milk to Sol lying on his side on the sofa. He has his arms wrapped around a throw pillow and his knees are curled up. I look at him and I hate what I think. I think, *Poor baby.*

I think, *Some day, we'll be good. We'll be good, brother.*

As if in response, he pulls himself up and takes the glass with both hands. He looks at me and his eyelids slip and he doesn't say anything until I begin to walk out of the room.

"I would probably wear that shirt," he says. "About the emptiness inside."

"I would too," I say, and open the cupboard, looking for a glass for myself.

CONTRIBUTORS

NICK BERTELSON's work has appeared in *The Coe Review*, *The Raleigh Review*, *Denver Syntax*, *The Big Stupid Review*, and others. He currently lives in Iowa.

TOM BONFIGLIO's stories have appeared or are forthcoming in over a dozen publications, including, *Fiction*, *Northwest Review*, *The Florida Review*, *Lake Effect*, *The Literary Review*, *Wag's Revue*, *Mixer* and *Unlikely Stories*. He won the Robert C. Martindale Prize in Long Fiction, and has received Special Mention in *The Pushcart Prizes: Best of the Small Presses*. He lives in Paradise Valley, Arizona.

JON MORGAN DAVIES is a native of California currently residing in Georgia and in cyberspace. His work has appeared in such publications as *Adirondack Review*, *Cutbank*, and *Southern Indiana Review*. Read more at www.no1bag.angelfire.com.

CURTIS DAWKINS is *BULL*'s chief book reviewer. He earned an M.F.A. from Western Michigan University and is currently an inmate at the Michigan Reformatory in Ionia, Michigan. His short story collection will be the first release forthcoming from BULL Books.

PATRICK HALEY lives and draws in Alaska.

JOSHUA KLEINBERG lives in Columbus, Ohio with his two cats, Necronomicat and Peachez. A full list of his publications can be found at joshuakleinberg.com.

CHUCK KLOSTERMAN is a contributing editor at Grantland and the author of five non-fiction books—*Fargo Rock City, Sex, Drugs, and Cocoa Puffs, Killing Yourself to Live, Chuck Klosterman IV,* and *Eating the Dinosaur*—and the novels *Downtown Owl* and *The Visible Man.*

SARA LIPPMANN's stories have appeared in *PANK, Our Stories, Jewish Fiction, Slice Magazine, Big Muddy, Potomac Review* and many other publications. She co-hosts the Sunday Salon, a monthly NYC reading series, and lives in Brooklyn with her family.

JAMES-ALEXANDER MATHERS' illustrations have been featured on GQ, Vanity Fair, and Urban Outfitters websites. He lives in Toronto.

DAN MICKLETHWAITE is a writer, painter, bedroom guitarist, and proud (though financially-challenged) owner of a Masters Degree in English Literature. He makes a large selection of his shorter fiction and poetry available online at his blog, but some has also appeared on *Ink, Sweat and Tears.* He lives in Yorkshire, England, where he is, as always, working on a novel.

PATRICK PARR currently lives with his wife in Leysin, Switzerland, where he teaches at Kumon Leysin Academy, an international school for Japanese high school students. His novel, *English as a Second Life,* is a finalist in the Clive Cussler Adventure Writer's Competition. Previous work has appeared in or been recognized by *Glimmer Train, The Storyteller, Skive Magazine,* among others.

PADGETT POWELL's latest book is *The Interrogative Mood*. His novel *Edisto* was nominated for the National Book Award, and his writing has appeared in *The New Yorker, Harper's, Paris Review, Esquire*; and has been anthologized in *Best American Short Stories* and *Best American Sportswriting*.

ETHEL ROHAN is the author of *Hard to Say* (PANK, 2011) and *Cut Through the Bone* (Dark Sky Books, 2010). Her work has or will appear in *World Literature Today, The Irish Times, The Chattahoochee Review, Los Angeles Review, Potomac Review* and *Southeast Review Online*, among many others. Raised in Dublin, Ireland, she now lives in San Francisco with her husband and two daughters.

JARED YATES SEXTON serves as Managing Editor of *BULL* and is an Assistant Professor of English at Ball State University. His first collection of stories, *An End to All Things*, will be released by Atticus Books in November 2012.

When he was a soldier, **RYAN GLENN SMITH** published dozens of articles for the United States Army about what a bang-up job we were doing in Iraq. But "Ventura" is the first published piece of fiction that he really enjoyed writing. He grew up in Memphis, Tennessee, a city with excellent tap water.

KEVIN WILSON is the author of a story collection, *Tunneling to the Center of the Earth* (Harper Perennial, 2009), and a novel, *The Family Fang* (Ecco, 2011). His short stories have appeared in *Ploughshares, Tin House, One Story, DIAGRAM*, and *The Collagist*. He lives in Sewanee, TN, and teaches fiction at The University of the South.

BULL
{salutes}

The following parties who helped make this issue and the
future of BULL possible.

Matt Bird

Ryan Bradley

Michael Buono

Coleman Collins

Dockers

Raul Jara

J.D. Smith

Peter Witte

Them's good folk.

BULLmensfiction.com

CPSIA information can be obtained at www.ICGtesting.com
Printed in the USA
LVOW070835130312

272846LV00001B/1/P